The Great Purple Hoo-Ha

A comedy of perception

★

Part One

★

By Philip H. Farber

Copyright © 2010 Philip H Farber & Mandrake

First Edition

Published by
Mandrake of Oxford
PO Box 250
OXFORD
OX1 1AP (UK)

This is a work of fiction. Names, characters, places and incidents either are the product of the author's imagination or are used fictitiously. Any resemblance to actual persons, living or dead, business establishments, events or locales is entirely coincidental. If you think otherwise, get over it.

All rights reserved. No part of this work may be reproduced or utilized in any form by any means electronic or mechanical, including *xerography, photocopying, microfilm,* and *recording,* or by any information storage system without permission in writing from the publishers.

Cover illustration by D J Reese

ISBN 978-1906958-169

For Robert Anton Wilson and A.J. Rose.

I wish you were here to see this.

1 ★ Joe's Show

Joe could sense the growing attention of the audience, the full engagement of the cameramen, and the increasing emotional involvement of his guest.

This is going to be good, he thought.

"We just want our daughter back," the woman sobbed. "We just want to get her out of there."

"For those who have just tuned in," Joe said in a subdued tone, "Mrs. Westheimer's nineteen-year-old daughter has joined – or been taken by? – a cult. Mrs. Westheimer, when did you last see or hear from your daughter?"

The woman dabbed at her eyes with a kleenex, smudging tear-soaked make-up. "It's been over a year now. They snatched her away just after her eighteenth birthday."

"You say they 'snatched her away,'" Joe pointed out. "Did they actually come and kidnap her?"

"I don't know what they did to convince her to go," Mrs. Westheimer moaned. "They warped her mind or brainwashed her or something. One day she was our sweet, charming daughter, the next she was a crazy person, spouting all these crazy ideas. Then when they came for her, she just climbed right into that car, even though we pleaded with her, even though we told her to stay."

Joe stroked his chin and looked thoughtful for a moment. "When did you first notice that she was falling under the ideological sway of this new religion?"

Mrs. Westheimer sniffled and choked back her next sob. "It started with little things. We'd find these cards and books around the house that said – I don't know – weird things on them."

"Such as?"

"Here. I've got one here." Mrs. Westheimer produced a cardboard square from a pocket and offered it to Joe.

The side facing Joe had three paragraphs of text in a clean but tiny san-serif font. He squinted at it and began to read out loud for the benefit of the audience. "The Invocation of Atem." He glanced up. "That's ay-tee-ee-em. Atem. It says: 'When your life is ready for a change, when things are bleak and getting bleaker, when your possibilities seem at an end – call on Atem. Atem is the Opener of the Way. He is your connection to the gods and goddesses of the ages, the demons and angels of the greater consciousness, the spirits and guides of the unseen world. Are you ready for your world to change?' It continues on for a bit more."

Joe brought his gaze up to include the audience, the viewers at home and the cue cards. "We've seen this stuff before," he said. "We've heard the phony gurus and preachers lay down this line of b.s. before. The appeal to the hopeless, to our friends and family members who are so down, so lost and confused that they will grasp at the tiniest twig of false hope that comes along. And the promise of otherworldly help, some blessing that will magically appear if you just donate all your worldly belongings or give away your free will or submit to whatever indignities they tell you to.

"Mrs. Westheimer, can you tell us? What was your daughter's life like when she was, hm, carried away by this?"

The woman wiped her eyes some more, the make-up now darkening her sockets, giving her a hollow, undead appearance which was belied by her pathetic tones and intermittent sobs. "She'd had her problems. What teen doesn't? But she was a sweet kid, really. Kind of nerdy, you know. She reads a lot, spends a lot of time on the computer, that kind of thing. Never very popular, really. She only had one date with a boy the whole time she was in high school. We should have been more worried after the incident with the drugs…"

Joe leaned in close. "Drugs?"

"The weed. We caught her smoking it in the basement."

"Okay, so let me get this right," Joe began as one of the cameras pulled in close. "She was a misfit? Maybe not as pretty as some of her friends? Spent a lot of time alone? Started turning to drugs?"

Mrs. Westheimer nodded.

"Did she ever express any thoughts about… suicide?"

"Suicide? No… I mean… She never said… Maybe… I don't know…If only we had encouraged her to open up more…" The sobs shook her whole body.

"It's okay, Mrs. Westheimer. We're not blaming you. But these cults are opportunistic. They're predators, feeding off the weak and sick members of society. They see a teen who is confused, desperate, and in trouble and they offer their so-called help. And they don't disclose the price until it's too late.

"So tell us, Mrs. Westheimer, what does this cult do? What do they believe?"

"Well that's the scary part," she said. "They devote their lives to the end of the world."

"The end of the world?"

"They pray to something. It's got a funny name. And when they pray to it enough, it's supposed to come and the world is supposed to end. I'm afraid…"

"What are you afraid of, Mrs. Westheimer?"

"I'm afraid they're all going to kill themselves."

Joe assumed an even more serious expression and held it silently for a moment so the cameras could soak it up. "This thing that's supposed to come: what is it? A UFO? A monster? A disaster of some kind?"

"I don't know. I just know they call it… they call it…"

"What do they call it?"

Her voice faltered. "The Great Purple Hoo-Ha."

The studio was silent for a moment. Then the audience exploded with laughter, a few catcalls puncturing the general commotion. Joe allowed it, looking deeply concerned and thoughtful until the disturbance passed its peak.

"That's really what they call it?" he asked. "The Great Purple Hoo-Ha?"

Mrs. Westheimer nodded meekly. "I said it had a funny name."

"What exactly is a Great Purple Hoo-Ha?"

She shook her head. "I don't know. But I'll tell you this: It's not the way we raised our daughter. We didn't raise her to believe in Hoo-Has of any color. We gave her a solid religious upbringing."

"What religion do you follow, Mrs. Westheimer?"

The sobs stopped and she looked up proudly. "We belong to the Original Orthodox Church of the Second Coming of Elvis."

The audience howled. Joe shouted over the noise. "We'll be right back after this message!"

2 ★ I Want To See Some Money

"That was awful." Jerry Hull was bald, corpulent, his voice marginally louder than the orange spots on his tie. "What the hell was that?"

"I thought it was pretty good," Joe said. "I really had 'em going there for a while. You could just feel the tension."

"Yeah, and then you let your guest speak. We loved her when she was a victim, not an idiot. And what was with that dress she had on?"

"Wardrobe picked it out," Joe said. "I thought it distracted from her... other features. I mean, a woman that size, what can you put her in?"

"Uh, huh. It was lousy TV, Joe. What's with these shows, anyway? Used to be, we had drag queen airline pilots and the spurned wives of polygamous politicians. Women who tore their clothes off and the one guy who tried to kill the cameraman with – what was that? A rubber fish? Now it's all cult-kid moms and school teachers who are witches. Who cares? I miss the good old days."

Joe looked up at Jerry. "We're only in our second season. And it was a dildo, not a rubber fish"

"The point is," Jerry continued, "is that it sucks. I hate to put it to you like this, Joe, 'cause you've been my friend forever - since we first met two and a half years ago, but something's gotta change with the show. Next week's show better knock me on my ass and pull some new ratings. And draw in a new sponsor. I want to see some money."

"We'll do our best. The crew always..."

"No, Joe. You'll do your best. Better than your best. Or we'll replace you."

Joe gulped. "Who would you replace me with?"

"Mark Layton."

"Mark Layton? Do you think Mark Layton is better looking than me?"

"He's taller than you, Joe, with broader shoulders, too. And he's got good hair."

Joe ran a hand over his professionally shellacked hair. "Better hair than mine?"

"I don't care about your goddamn hair, Joe! Honestly, I've always had my doubts about you. I thought you were too damn wishy washy and, you know, kind of foul. I just want to see some exciting TV for a change! Okay? Next week." Jerry paused for a moment and then added a pleading whine to his voice. "Please, Joe?"

Joe ran his fingers over his craggy face. "I... Yes, Jerry. I'll figure something out."

"Okay, then," Jerry suddenly grinned. "We gonna go grab some sushi and Brazilian girls, like you suggested?"

"No," Joe said, his voice a weak echo of his professional standard. "I don't think I'm hungry."

3 ✶ Invocation of Atem

Joe wrapped a black trench coat over his on-air suit and wandered out into the evening. Gray clouds and twilight loomed over a city that pulsed and roared. To Joe's ears, though, the background throb of New York faded as an internal voice-over soundtrack played louder and louder.

"They don't like me," Joe's mind yammered. "They see me on TV and what I do isn't good enough. I'm not as good as all the other crap on the air. How humiliating is that?"

Now, Joe had been in therapy and knew he had some "issues" about recognition and approval. But this was more than some issues. Jerry didn't like him. This was for real. They didn't like him, the people who watched, the people he did all this for. Their approval — it was what he was here for, what he lived for, what motivated him to get up in the morning and glue down his hair and go to work.

"They don't like me. They don't like me. I suck I suck I suck."

There was only one place to go now.

The liquor store was a beacon of colored lights, backlit amber, green and red liquids behind a thick glass window. Just looking at the bottles in the window, Joe could feel the numbness creeping in, hear the inner voice quieting down or at least slurring until unintelligible. Inside, a surly cashier swiped Joe's Visa card and handed over a quart of Old Mystery in a brown paper bag. Joe pocketed his card and unsealed the cap of the bottle with a firm twist.

"C'mon, guy," the cashier complained. "Wait 'til you get outside, okay?"

Two hours later, Joe was halfway through the O.M., but there wasn't nearly as much relief as he had anticipated. His inner voice was only a bit quieter, but now much whinier and was complaining about itself.

"What a fucking whiner," Joe's inner voice bitched. "I really suck. Why do I do this to myself? Why don't I just shut the fuck up?"

He tried to napalm the voice with another big gulp of O.M. The booze seared his throat and the bottle clinked sharply as he banged it back down to the concrete. Joe wouldn't be caught dead serving O.M. to his professional friends, but it was just the stuff to dull nerve endings and burn out key brain cells in a hurry.

Joe wasn't quite sure where he was. He was sitting in a doorway on a dark street of warehouses or factories or something. During the day, the narrow avenue would bustle with trucks and blue collar guys. Now the well-dressed and fairly wasted white guy was a roadside attraction for the few odd pedestrians who wandered by.

"Look at me," Joe thought. "What a fucking loser. They don't like me at all."

Another big, burning slug of O.M. and bang went the bottle back onto the concrete step. This time it didn't clink so much as it crashed, shattering on the pavement.

"Fuck," thought Joe. "What a fuck up. I can't even get fucking wasted without fucking up."

He climbed shakily to his feet, brushing shards of broken glass from the trench coat. He reached into the coat and checked his suit pocket to make sure he was armed with his Visa card for another foray to the liquor store.

But his hand didn't close around plastic. It closed around a piece of cardboard. He pulled it out and squinted at it in the dim light. There were a few paragraphs of tiny text. At the top it said: "The Invocation of Atem."

"It's a tiny little cue card," Joe said.

The Invocation of Atem

When your life is ready for a change, when things are bleak and getting bleaker, when your possibilities seem at an end – call on Atem. Atem is the Opener of the Way. He is your connection to the gods and goddesses of the ages, the demons and angels of the greater consciousness, the spirits and guides of the unseen world. Are you ready for your world to change? Say the following out loud:

I offer my attention, the force of my consciousness, to Atem. I do this by speaking these words and allowing my understanding of them to develop. I charge these words with my emotions, with the power of my wants and needs, the feelings of my gains and losses, my joy, sorrow, love, anger, enthusiasm, melancholy, and elation. I start right where I am now, with the things I have close to hand, the thoughts and tools that already fit into my life. I ask that my experience of the world can change so that I can better make use of my thoughts and tools. I hope to notice you, Atem, in every way that you manifest in my life.

Now be open to Atem's forms. Thoughts and manifestations of Atem may occur near bodies of water in the sunlight, or in places that are sacred to computers and information technology, or where the setting sun shines through trees, or at night where people socialize and explore each other's dreams and desires, or in any other place where the complexity of interaction reaches beyond the ability of a human's conscious mind. Atem lives on the border of chaos, where the butterfly's wing beats, where graphs become asymptotic, and in that place where William Blake saw infinity in a grain of sand. Atem is not here to save the Earth or unite mankind or to put health, wealth, and wisdom in your hand. Atem is here to Open the Way for the diversity of entities who are capable of those tasks – and much more.

As Joe reached the end of the short text, he realized that he had been reading out loud. And not just out loud; he had read the words on the little card in a slightly manic, definitely drunken version of his on-air voice. He glanced up and down the street, to make sure he was alone. Two young couples walking together on the opposite side of the street stared with horror and disgust.

"Ah, screw it," Joe said. "I fucked up again." And he set off in search of booze.

4 ✷ Adam

The liquor store was closed, but a bar up the block was open, spilling a muted yellow glow and a thin trickle of rock music from its opening door. It was warm inside, with a reek of fermentation not entirely from the beverages. A neglected jukebox in the corner mumbled tunes that were meant to be shouted and mumbling seemed a trend among the clientele as well. A bouncer lounging near the door eyed Joe skeptically and then returned to his torpor. Joe found a place to lean and slapped his Visa on the bar top. A zaftig hooker in a tight pink dress appraised his shoes and apparently decided against pitching her wares. Soon he had a pisswater beer and a triple shot of O.M. in hand and was navigating an indirect course to a vacant booth.

In the next booth, two women in dark suits were exchanging locked briefcases with a short scruffy black man. At a table not far away, a young couple, barely old enough to be in a bar, pawed at each other's clothing and bathed each other in slobbery, drunken kisses. The girl's left breast had mostly emerged from her blouse and her hand circled repeatedly toward the boy's bulging crotch. At the bar the hooker was telling stories to two ancient hardcore alkies. They mumbled to each other and laughed. The jukebox droned a whiney grunge number from the 1990s.

Joe noticed very little of this. He gulped at his drinks and wallowed in boozy self-loathing. His life played before his eyes in dark, grainy retrospective footage as the voice-over track continued berating every act, quality, and manifestation of his being. And, indeed, as Joe reviewed his recent career, it now seemed small, sordid and, generally, a seriously disturbing mistake.

"Life fuckin' sucks," Joe mumbled.

He barely noticed when someone slid into the booth next to him, plunking a cardboard coaster and a beer glass onto the table.

"What's that you say?" a voice asked.

Joe looked up to see a young man holding a large gray cat. The man appeared to be in his middle twenties, slim with unruly black hair. His clothes – a threadbare sweater and stained jeans – seemed quite appropriate for the locale. He looked healthy. Indeed, he seemed to glow with health. And his cat seemed unusually large and expressive, luminous yellow-green eyes scanning Joe with a calm gaze. The young man's presence was sobering in a way, just enough to pull Joe the tiniest bit from his inner morass.

"Fuck you," Joe said, surprising himself with his own clarity and enunciation.

"Say, aren't you that guy from TV," the man said, "Joe… Schmoe?"

"Fuck you," Joe repeated. "It's 'Joe's Show,' asshole. My name is Joe Maloney."

Joe gulped the last of his O.M.

"Hey," the young man said, "I'll get you another."

"Yeah, all right." Joe sucked beer and in a moment another glass of booze was aromatically present. O.M. followed the beer on a short journey to Joe's interior.

"Having a bad night, are you?" The young man asked. "You know, I'm here to help."

"Fuck you. Whatever you're selling, I'll listen as long as you're buying. Hell, maybe not even that long. I can afford my own damn booze. I'm not a fucking mark."

"Oh, no, Joe," the man said. "I'm not selling anything. I just want your attention for a little while. And I'm going to change your life."

"I'm not buying anything. I'm not going anywhere with you. I'm just sitting right here with my Old Mystery."

"That's right. Hey, I've seen a few of your shows. They were cool."

"The show fucking sucks. Everyone knows it. Except me."

"I thought it was fun. The one where the guy tried to kill the cameraman with – what was that? – a live eel?"

"Old news," Joe mumbled. "Everything's gone downhill. The show sucks. I suck. This fucking bar sucks. The booze doesn't suck. You suck. Your fucking cat sucks. And it was a rubber fish, not a fucking eel."

"You seem much friendlier and slightly more articulate on the show."

"Fuck you."

"Enough of this." The man waved the conversation away like a bad fart. "Time to get down to business."

Joe drank deeply. "Here comes the sales pitch."

"Would it make a difference if you knew my name was Atem?"

"Nice to fucking meet you, Adam. So, c'mon, tell me already. What are you selling?"

"Again, Joe, I'm going to give you something, but first I need you to be ready for it, and I really just need your full attention for a moment. So maybe we can start where your attention is already aimed. It hurts, doesn't it? It hurts to think your show sucks."

Joe winced. "Fuck you."

"It hurts to think that *you* suck, doesn't it?"

Joe almost doubled over with pain.

Atem began to speak in a quiet, rhythmic voice. "Notice where in your body you feel the pain, Joe. Notice where the feeling starts. The more you think about how bad your life sucks, you can notice how the feeling grows and moves. Think about what Jerry told you. Think about Jerry. He doesn't like you, he just likes the money. It's not about you. You're insignificant. You suck, Joe. Now notice where the feeling moves to. Pay attention to what kind of a feeling it is. There are all kinds of feelings – tingling, pressure, temperature, movement, texture. If the feeling had a color, what would it be?"

"Kind of a brownish, black, shiny color," Joe mumbled. "Ugh."

"Good, good," Atem said. "Now notice how the feeling, the color, cycles. As you breathe, it pulses or it cycles. Can you notice that?"

Joe nodded and gestured with his hand, a circular movement toward the center of his body.

"Okay, Joe, now take a deep breath and as you do so, reverse the direction of the feeling. Make it cycle the other way. *Turn things around.*"

Joe took a deep breath and suddenly sat up very straight. His left eye opened a bit wider. "That's very odd," he said.

"Feel a little different now?" Atem asked.

"Yeah," said Joe. "It's weird, but, yeah, I do."

"How did the feeling change?"

Joe thought for a moment. "When it changed direction, it also changed color. It turned sort of gold and bright. Before it was sort of dragging me down. Now it feels like it lifts me up. And the voice is gone."

"Okay," Atem continued. "Now keep it moving in the new direction. Make the colors richer, make it larger, make it move through more and more of your body."

Joe was still listing to one side, but both eyes were now equally open.

"Perfect!" Atem exclaimed. "Awake enough now to pay attention to me for a few minutes?"

"You know, Adam, I think I am. You've got my attention. I can't believe you just did that."

"Actually, you did that," Atem said, his cat turning around and nestling peacefully in his lap. "I just gave you a little nudge. Now I'm going to help you with your little career problem – and maybe a bit more. And in the process, you might be helping me, too."

"Are you going to pitch me a show idea? Hell, I'll listen."

"Nothing that obvious," Atem said. "Have a drink, make yourself comfortable. I'm just going to tell you a little story."

Joe took a sip and leaned back against the cracked vinyl of the booth.

16 ✱ The Great Purple Hoo-Ha

5 ✶ The Most Disgusting Rock Star Ever

Atem wet his mouth with beer and his conversational tone changed just the tiniest bit, shifting down a little lower and slower. "Do you know who Rex Massenclear is?

"Sure," said Joe. "The musician. He had that hit song a few years back... What was that called?"

"Yo Momma Smoked My Blunt."

"No way."

"Yes, indeed. That's the song title."

"Massenclear... Wasn't he the guy who...?"

"Yes."

"Yes?"

"There are thousands of stories about Rex Massenclear and many of them are true or at least true enough. He is, in fact, the Most Disgusting Rock Star Ever. But before we get much further into this particular story, we need a little background music. Do you know about the Astral Score?"

"The what?"

Atem cocked his head as if he heard something in the distance, beyond the rustling and mumbling of the bar. "Listen. Life has a soundtrack, a score composed of harmonics, resonance, and interference patterns. Music that sounds just like a movie score. Most people can't hear it. They don't even know about it. Listen. Listen closely. You might be able to hear it. You have to be in a unique frame of mind to hear it the first time. Maybe it just needs your attention to even exist at all. Maybe it exists only in our imaginations, a metaphor in music for the myriad unconscious stimuli that surround us, defining the theme of the moment, the heart of the character. Doesn't matter. Once you've heard it, it's always there. Now listen. Just like in a movie, you'll hear the foley, the sound effects, the voices, the sound beds – and then over the top of that, the score." He tapped his ear with a finger. "Just listen."

Joe listened. The bar was full of the usual bar noises. Voices, glasses, the rhythmic noise of the underwhelming jukebox. And maybe something else floating just over that. Faintly.

"Listen," said Atem. "It's low now. Kind of a creepy, drunken science fiction B-movie theme. Building now a little."

"Yes," said Joe. "That's really weird. I've never heard that before."

The Astral Score swelled with volume, an undulating Theremin inviting entry into a world of boozed-out weirdness.

"So let me tell you about Rex Massenclear," Atem continued. "He was a middle-class kid who worshipped cars and Playboy bunnies, but drove a shitter and could never get a real date. He listened to music constantly, on the stereo, on MTV, on the radio in his crappy car. Rock'n'roll all day long. And he wanted to be a rock star. He wanted it really bad."

Atem leaned in close. His cat looked up and a drum fill underscored his seriousness. "Rex would have sold his soul for rock'n'roll."

As the drums rolled, Joe had a moment of panic. Is that what this was about? A deal with the devil? Joe made an effort to dismiss the thought, but ominous music, loopy Theremin and rough edged guitar, resumed as Atem returned to his tale.

"In fact, Rex tried to sell his soul. He borrowed books on black magick from the public library. He was almost hit by a truck as he waited in the crossroads at midnight. But it seemed that the market for souls like his was not very favorable. Every heavy metal kid with a rock star dream was willing to deal with the devil. And, mainly, there didn't seem to actually be a soul-buying devil anywhere around.

"So Rex tried to do it the hard way, with guitar lessons, practice and high school garage bands. He learned chords. He wrote songs. That's when he wrote 'Yo Momma,' when he was seventeen years old. He rehearsed and played gigs in the school gymnasium and the local Elks hall. But, of course, he never really did have much talent and it was all a waste of time.

"Then Rex had an epiphany. Well, actually he had an acid trip, but while he was grinning at the pulsation of a potted Fichus in his bass player's apartment, something interesting occurred to him. Actually, first what happened was that he farted. He cut a long, cheesy, nasty smelling boomer. He and his friends laughed until it hurt, enveloped in ass-fumes, and the laughter was so good, so wonderful, that Rex wanted to dwell in it forever. From Massenclear's unique frame of reference at that moment, it was a revelation, a sign concerning the ultimate direction of his life.

"He made a decision at that moment, a plan of action. If he could show his audience something of themselves; if they looked at him and could really relate, he'd have them hooked.

"Usually when we look at a rock star or a celebrity, we see something of who we want to be, some ideal form of ourselves, someone we can emulate and be like. We live vicariously through our media heroes. We loved Elvis because he was just a regular kid who could really sing. When we watched or listened to Elvis, we knew, just a little bit, what it felt like to be so cool. We wanted to be him and we lived the life through him. And simply doing this would change us, make deep changes to our neurology that influence our fundamental presuppositions about the world.

"Even in the case of drunkenness or drug abuse – Keith Richards, for instance – these are still traits that the average rock fan, in a way, admires. Keith Richards does it for us and we can dream about being that free or bold or fearless or batshit crazy or whatever. We see in these people some parts of ourselves that yearn to act that way, that *would* act batshit crazy if we had the money or time or groupies to do it.

"Rex cut one, his world was remade anew, and he decided he'd do the rock star thing in a slightly different way. His plan was not to show people the repressed free and bold aspects of themselves; rather he wanted to show people the parts of themselves that disgusted them. There are some things we hide away in our unconscious mind that, given the choice, we would want to set free – our creativity, our passion, our love, our spirituality. There are some repressed parts of consciousness that, given the choice, we would probably still choose to hide away: the stuff we do that grosses even ourselves out, our insufficiencies, our embarrassments, the parts of ourselves that we keep hidden from others at all costs. There have been a few celebrities who exposed some of that to a small extent, though more often by accident rather than by design. Sid Vicious, for instance, or Ozzy."

A heavy metal guitar riffed astrally.

Joe scratched his head. "Why would anyone…?"

Atem continued on. "Perhaps seeing it in someone else makes it safer for us. If we can watch Rex Massenclear pick his nose and hide it under the chair, it makes it just that much less disgusting when we actually find ourselves doing the same thing. Or perhaps it's like picking at a scab, it hurts a little, feels kind of nasty, and you know it must be unsanitary, but you just want to keep at it."

"I'm sorry, it's disgusting no matter what," Joe slobbered. "Is that how he managed it? By picking his nose in public?"

"Picking his nose, saying foul things, farting, scratching his ass, drooling copiously, spitting, coughing up substances of varying texture and consistency, among many other indulgences, some much more disgusting," Atem replied. "But those were just the most outward forms. Even if he was just sitting here, doing nothing at all, we'd still find him disgusting, annoying, and foul. It goes even deeper with him – or more accurately, it's so superficial that it's a thing of power."

There was a brief astral guitar solo and Atem sipped from his beer. Joe was slack-jawed, staring at Atem.

"So how did he go about doing this?" Joe was finally forced to ask.

"He started out as you'd expect, adding a geek act to his rock show. He'd curse and spit and blow his nose without a kleenex. He'd drool and get wasted and fall down and barf on himself. He'd pretend to crap his pants and smear it around. He developed a small following, but it never quite went anywhere. That is…"

Atem paused as the Theremin returned.

"Yes?" Joe prompted.

"It never went anywhere until Rex made a deal."

"I thought you said the Devil wasn't in the market," Joe said.

Atem stroked his cat nonchalantly. "He made a deal with me."

The Great Purple Hoo-Ha

6 ✶ It's Already Done

Joe took a gulp of his long-forgotten O.M. His mind was whirling faster than a drunk mind should whirl and it was making him a little dizzy. It took him a few minutes to articulate a thought.

"Is that the deal you're about to offer me?" Joe finally asked. "To make me The Most Disgusting TV Host Ever?" He thought for a moment. "I could do that."

"No," said Atem. "That's not it at all. In fact, I'm going to offer you the exact opposite. You see, Rex Massenclear was, before it all, a nice, normal guy. He was a little bit artsy, however untalented and unremarkable. He was basically nice. You, on the other hand, are fairly disgusting in your natural condition. You hide it under nice clothes and with cue-card-written words – but in reality, you are a self-obsessed, vain, crude, lowlife. You turn into a mean and - may I say it? - disgusting drunk in the face of even the slightest criticism. You really do suck, it's true."

"That's what I've been telling myself all evening," Joe said. "If only there was a way to guarantee that when people look at me, they see only good, only nobility. I could save my career. I could live with that."

"Wow! I've never heard the Astral Score quite this schmaltzy," Atem remarked. "Anyway, I wonder when you'll notice that it's already done, that you have already changed."

"What's already done?"

"It's almost what you said," Atem explained. "When people look at you, they'll see only good, only nobility. Hell, they'll see much more than that. They'll see you *doing* things that you never did, hear you *saying* things that you never said. However, the qualities and actions that they attribute to you are their own ideals, not necessarily yours. When someone sees you, they will see their own idea of what a good guy might be. Got it?"

"Riiight," Joe drawled. "Uh huh."

"You'll figure it out." Atem looked at his wristwatch. "It's just about time for this hallucination to end. Got any last questions before I go?"

"Yeah," said Joe. "Whatever happened to Rex Massenclear? I haven't heard anything about him in years."

"He retired from the music business and lives alone in a trailer in the Mojave Desert. He made enough money in two years of celebrity to live comfortably like that for the rest of his life."

"It's not what I would do if I had that kind of money or fame."

"You won't be The Most Disgusting Rock Star Ever. You'll probably be The Most Amazing TV Host Ever. You will undoubtedly chart a different course. Okay, I'm going now. Enjoy the rest of your evening. Remember to drink a lot of water." Atem got to his feet, shifting the cat under his arm.

"Thanks, Adam," Joe said. "It's been real."

"Has it?" Atem turned and strolled out to the music of astral guitars.

7 ✶ The First Morning

Joe woke in his own bed a little after eleven the next morning. His head was throbbing and his mouth tasted like stale vomit. After a delightfully gut-wrenching experience in the bathroom, he ended up in the kitchen, sipping weak coffee and moaning.

All was quiet. There was no Astral Score to accompany his groans. A few dimly remembered experiences from the previous evening served to convince Joe that he had endured some kind of alcohol-fueled hallucination, something like a psychedelic experience, except blurry and not fully crossing from memory to recollection.

"At least I didn't black out this time," he thought.

He followed the coffee with vitamins, headache pills and a glass of tap water. His belly made a plaintive cry and he realized that he'd have to get some food in him, too, but the quarantined containers of mold in his refrigerator were no help. He crawled into what remained of his clothing from the previous night and went down the stairs to the street.

When "Adam" spoke to him, his inner voice had shut up and had stayed mostly quiet. Now that he caught a whiff of himself as he walked, some fresh self-criticism began to gear up.

He began to list his recent hits: bad TV, emotional difficulties, over-consumption of O.M., a complete freak-out of some kind with both visual and auditory hallucinations, dirty clothing, a foul odor, a brain-slamming hangover. It was amazing they let people like him walk the street freely.

Maybe they were about to revoke that right. All along the street, passersby were staring at him.

"What?" he thought. "Was my little freak-out on the news or something?"

He tried to hunch down into himself as he hurried to a nearby coffeeshop.

An overly-friendly waitress brought him coffee and a breakfast special, even though it was already noon. The smell of strong coffee cleared his head a little and a few forkfuls of scrambled egg roused his appetite.

Someone at a nearby table must have had their walkman turned up too loud; a little bit of music, a warped polka, mingled with the clatter of dishes and the babble of voices.

The waitress kept circling back to his table, checking to make sure he was okay, asking if he needed anything. She topped off his coffee repeatedly, taking opportunities to lean in close and mash a breast against Joe's shoulder. The smell of grill grease and cheap perfume made him a little queasy. He belched an acid bubble of coffee and egg, attempting to hide the operation behind a napkin.

It didn't deter the waitress and she circled back around. "Hey, aren't you that guy from TV?" she asked. "Joe... Schmoe?"

"Joe Maloney," he croaked. "It's 'Joe's Show.'"

"You're even better looking in person," she giggled and hustled away.

"You're even crazier than I am," Joe mumbled at her retreating hindquarters.

Back out on the street he turned up his trench coat collar and tried to hide his stubbly face. People kept looking at him and smiling anyway. He paused at a street corner, waiting for the light to change, and a beautiful woman gave him a dazzling grin. His dehydrated brain strained to think of something to say, but he came up empty and crossed the street in silence.

As he reached the opposite side, the woman caught up with him. She looked at him shyly. "I just wanted to say what a nice thing that was."

"Excuse me?"

"I mean, a person of your stature," the woman said, "even noticing someone like me. That was such a kind thing to say."

"What did I say?" Joe was genuinely confused.

"Oh, now you're just being modest," the woman said.

"That's right," said an older woman who had stopped to listen. "You're a very kind young man. I saw what you did."

"Kind isn't even the half of it," the first woman said, now flirting openly.

"Whoa!" called a young black man, suddenly joining the street corner group. "Aren't you that guy from TV? Joe…"

"Yeah, Joe Maloney," Joe said, extending a hand to shake away the inevitable Schmoe. "'Joe's Show'"

"Well, damn," the man said. "You're one of my heroes."

"I am?"

"You are now! Now I see why you get the big bucks. Damn!"

"Okay, thank you everyone," Joe said, a hint of his professional voice creeping in. "But it's really time for me to go."

He turned and brusquely shouldered his way through the expanding group. Somewhere nearby there was music playing, urban and funky with just a little bit of old sci-fi Theremin. He stopped suddenly and scanned the block, but all he could see was the group of new-found fans, closing in on him. Joe pulled his coat up over his aching head and marched doubletime back to his building. He made sure the heavy outer security door locked tight, proceeded up to his apartment and bolted the door behind him.

He turned on the TV and dialed the news. He flipped open his laptop computer and googled his own name. Nothing. Not a mention beyond the usual sites. There was the official show site, a slew of specific show references on a variety of forums, none of them more recent than last week, and his Kiwipedia entry:

> **Joseph P. Maloney**, known to the public simply as **Joe** or **Joe Schmoe** is the host of a syndicated television talk show, *Joe's Show*. A professional actor who also worked as a plumber's assistant, Maloney achieved notoriety after portraying a beer-obsessed psychologist in a series of television commercials for Merkin brand beer. After filling in for other commentators, Maloney joined the POX News team, delivering an "opinion rant" weekly for over two years.
>
> One of his most well-known rants advocated the use of wiretapping and other espionage methods by U.S. government agencies to spy freely and without regulation on other U.S. government agencies and officials. The reasoning went, "That will keep them busy and the rest of us can get on with our lives."

Maloney is currently the host of *Joe's Show*, a weekly talk show known for outrageous themes and occasional on-air nudity and violence. The show received a Flatus Award, given to the best of television talk format programming, for an episode in which a guest attacked a cameraman with a large, dripping pastry.

Joe's Show has garnered only moderate ratings. Critics of Maloney's work suggest that the spontaneous-seeming aspects are actually scripted and that Maloney "sometimes stumbles over the longer words written on his cue cards."

Nothing had been changed or added and there were no news releases or even anything that might suggest a healthy viewing audience. There was simply nothing at all to explain why he had suddenly seemed the celebrity of the moment out there on the street. Maybe it was something about him. Maybe he had just hit that right combination of gritty and grimy and real. Or maybe he had accidentally discovered the key to fame through disgust, like – what was his name? – Rex Massenclear.

But... Rex hadn't found the key accidentally... He... made a deal with that guy Adam?

Did Adam really do something? He had to find out. He flipped out his cell phone and called Jerry Hull.

"Jerry? Is there anything I should know about? Some publicity that hit? A review? A piece?"

"Joe? What's going on? No, absolutely no publicity on that last, sorry show of yours, thank god. But what's up with you? You sound really good. You're working on something, aren't you?"

"Really? No publicity? Yeah, yeah, I'm working. Thanks." And Joe hung up.

"Okay," he said out loud. "Let's test this thing out."

Joe checked himself in the mirror. His eyes were deeply bloodshot, his forehead creased with pain, and a day's worth of stubble covered his face. Joe's normally glued-down hair-do was a tangled mess of wannabe dreadlocks. He looked pale, he smelled bad, and his black trench coat was dusty and rumpled.

"Perfect," he thought and marched back down the stairs and out to the street.

Faintly, somewhere in the distance, French horns began to play.

8 ✷ Make Mine a Merkin

Joe's eyes took a moment to focus on the sunlit street. A skinny, ragged man was lounging nervously outside Joe's door. His clothes were filthier than Joe's and his eyes had a crazy, far-away look that said "crackhead."

"Hey, do you have a few dollars you can spare?" The man spoke in a high-pitched whine. "I took the bus in to New York now I don't have any money and I just need the doo-fifty to get home to New Jersey. You know Hoboken? I gotta catch the bus, man. C'mon man…" At that point the man actually looked up at Joe. "Hey! I know you! Aren't you that guy from TV? Joe… Something?"

"Yeah, that's me."

"I knew it, man! And you know you got that look, man. You been smoking some serious shit, I can tell. Got a hit for a friend?"

"No," said Joe. "You are one fucked up person, you know that?"

"Yeah," the man said. "I know. I wish I could be like you, Joe, to have control. To smoke some shit and still stand up straight and have a job and shit."

"Fucking crackhead," Joe said, lengthening his stride.

"Thank you, Joe," the fucking crackhead whined. "That's some good advice. I could do that… You know…"

Joe left him behind and popped in to a Korean market. He wandered past a long steamtable of reeking delicacies to the refrigerator and mentally debated whether a beer would help or hinder him. On the pro side of the argument, it would be cool, refreshing and might provide much-needed Hair of the Dog. On the con side – well, there wasn't much of a con side. Two adolescent girls in the candy isle were nudging each other and staring. He smiled and waved and instead of fleeing in horror as they should have, they giggled and waved back shyly.

Joe grabbed a can of Merkin and made his way to the checkout where the Korean man behind the counter insisted loudly that he take the beer for free. "It is an honor for us that you come in here," the counterman said. "Maybe soon you come back so we can take a picture of you, hang it on the wall here." He pointed to a cluttered spot on the wall where racks of condoms and rolling papers vied for space with a signed eight by ten photograph of a local ball player.

Out on the street, Joe popped open the beer and took a long swig. The flash flood of liquid in his parched throat swept away phlegm and dust and the leftover flavors of breakfast. After a moment – and half the can – it began to erode his pain, smoothing the sharp edges off the hangover. Joe looked up to find a uniformed police officer staring at him.

Joe usually had at least token respect for New York's open container law and did what everyone else did; he hid his bottle or can in a brown paper bag. But in his haste to gift Joe with the beer, the cashier hadn't provided a bag. Joe looked at the beer and then up at the cop.

"You really do drink Merkin," the cop commented. "That's so cool."

"Uh, yeah."

"*Make mine a Merkin!*" the cop recited the tag line from the old commercial.

"Right."

"You know, you always wonder when a celebrity endorses some regular kind of product. Did Florence Henderson really use that cooking oil? Did Lorne Greene taste the Alpo? Did the Sex Pistols drink Mountain Dew? Does the Hawaiian Bikini Team really have sex with guys who drink Schmuck Beer? Hell, do you think the guy in the Ronald McDonald suit actually eats that crap? Well, now we know you are a man of integrity. Joe Schmoe really drinks Merkin!"

"Fuck you," said Joe.

"You're welcome." The cop smiled benignly.

An astral horn section was growing louder and Joe decided to push it a little. "Eat me, you fucking pig," he said.

"That's my job," the cop smiled.

Joe smiled back. "I said, 'Eat me, you fucking pig.'"

"Oh yes, and I really appreciate it. It's so rare for a citizen of your stature to offer useful feedback to a beat cop like me. And you really do drink Merkin. I've gotta say, you made my day. Thanks, Joe."

"Thank you, officer. You really made my day, too."

The horns were rising to a fanfare as Joe strode off, sipping beer.

# The Great Purple Hoo-Ha

9 ✷ The Mirror Girl

Back home, Joe sucked the last warm gulp of beer. He cleared debris from his sofa and lay down to think. *Something had certainly changed.* He felt the same, which is to say, horrible, dirty and full of self-loathing. But people were responding to him differently. Now a crackhead, a cashier and a cop weren't definitive proof of anything, he realized. He could still be imagining this.

No, that cop should have kicked his ass. Would have, if Joe wasn't, somehow, different.

The creepy Theremin theme had returned.

And then there was that: the music. The Astral Score? What kind of nutball bullshit was that? But nonetheless…

More Theremin; staccato percussion.

"Ah, fuck it," Joe mumbled. This was way too much thought for his hangover-addled brain to handle. He stuffed a pillow under his head and passed out.

When he woke again it was evening. The hangover was somewhat in remission and Joe was ravenously hungry. It took ten minutes to convince a garrulous pizza delivery boy to hand him the box and leave. Joe ate half a pie, belched thoroughly, and then rested before a long, hot shower.

Drying himself off, he contemplated the second chance that seemed to have dropped in his unworthy lap. The cautionary aspect was obvious. If he really developed and used this – talent? ability? quirk? – he could end up running and hiding from crowds of adoring fans, like a real celebrity. He would be isolated. Insulated. There would be blacked-out limos and private entrances, bodyguards and security. He would have gofers and front men, groupies and stalkers.

"I can handle that," he said out loud. "It would be a small price to pay."

First, though, he needed to know more. He needed to know just what he could and couldn't do. He needed to know how to really *use* this thing. He needed to find the source, that guy with the cat, Adam. Joe grabbed his coat and went out into the night.

The bar seemed brighter and just slightly less dismal than it had through the previous night's alcoholic haze. Muffled rock music rose from the jukebox like the aroma of rancid beer from the sticky floor. Some of the patrons looked familiar, though it was difficult for Joe to recall. The one person he would have recognized, Adam, was nowhere to be seen.

Joe slid up to the bar and was greeted heartily by a pale and wrinkly bartender. He ordered a draft beer. "Do you happen to recall the man I was talking to last night?" Joe asked the gnome-like server.

"Were you in here last night?" the bartender puzzled. "I think I would have remembered that. You're that guy from TV, right?"

"Right."

A lone astral saxophone began to play. Joe felt a hand on his shoulder and he turned hopefully to find that it was not Adam, but a buxom hooker overflowing a thin pink dress. Black hair was piled on her head in a vintage Tina Turner do and smooth, café au lait skin drew Joe's eye toward a Grand Canyon of cleavage that almost, but not quite disappeared into the dress. She had a bit of padding pretty much everywhere, yet it all added up to "voluptuous," just this side of "too much."

"Joe Maloney, right?" she asked.

"That's me," Joe said, momentarily impressed by the lack of Schmoe.

"I'm a fan," the woman said. "Marlena." She thrust out a soft hand and captured one of Joe's in a quick handshake. "I just love the show. That episode where the guy attacked the cameraman with a dildo, that was simply hysterical. I can't remember the last time I'd laughed so hard."

"A dildo," Joe said. "You caught that?"

"I don't miss much," she said, scanning him suggestively from head to toe.

"Good," Joe nodded enthusiastically. "That's good. Were you here in the bar last night, Marlena?"

"Right here."

"Do you remember who I was talking to last night?"

"Were you here last night? I think I would have remembered that."

Joe pointed to the booth. "I was sitting right there and I was talking to a young man who had a cat. A big gray cat."

"No way," Marlena said. "There was just some old derelict over there, talking to himself for half the night."

"No, really. I was sitting there. And there was someone with me. I need to find him."

"I just remember the old bum," she said. "And I wasn't too drunk or anything. Business was slow; I was here almost all night."

"Hmmm, right." Joe thought for a moment. "The old bum, what was he wearing?"

"Lessee," Marlena's eyes drifted up to the ceiling as she recalled. "An old black trench coat... and dirty dress slacks... and... black leather shoes with barf or something on them."

"Like this?" Joe gestured at his own old, dirty and barfed-on ensemble.

"Like that, sure," Marlena said. "But disgusting. You look sharp. Sexy. Working your assets in a big way. Totally different."

"Okay, okay," Joe said. "Did the bum have anyone with him?"

"Not that I saw. He was just mumbling to himself. Got real excited a couple times, too. But maybe someone else saw you." She turned and leaned down the bar toward two withered old men who were drinking and watching silently. "Hey Bob. Hey, Tim. Did you see Joe here last night?"

"That's Joe?" asked Bob.

"Joe Schmoe," said Tim.

"Was he here last night?" Bob asked.

"I think I would have remembered that," Tim said.

Marlena turned back to Joe and shrugged.

"Oh well," said Joe. "I was a little out of it last night. Maybe I'm not recalling things correctly."

"Oh, I'm sure your memory is just fine," Marlena assured him. "This guy – how come you're looking for him?"

"Well... he gave me something that... I think it's going to change my life."

"Was he distributing religious literature? The management doesn't hold with that. Bad enough he brought a live animal into a place where food is served."

"No," Joe said. "He wasn't distributing literature. He said he just wanted my attention."

Marlena nodded. "That's what it's all about."

"What?"

"Attention."

"You lost me," said Joe. "That's what it's all about?"

"Sure, everyone needs attention, everyone gives attention. It's really all we have. I learned that from Wilderman."

There was an astral fanfare played on electric guitar.

"Wilderman?"

Again the guitar fanfare.

"A business acquaintance. He said that everything is defined by attention."

"What does that mean?"

"I'll show you." She pinched the nipple of her left breast through the thin fabric of the dress and gave the magnificent mammary a jiggle. Astral drums played a solo. Joe could do nothing except watch in fascination as the Grand Canyon endured an earthquake and several aftershocks. His blood filled with hormones and the concoction migrated south. Every part of his attention was pointed in the same direction. After a moment he remembered to look back up at her face.

"Got your attention, did I?" she grinned.

"That was impressive," he said.

"Thank you. Now the attention we are giving each other has defined our relationship in a new and different way. The question is, once we have each other's attention, where do we lead it?"

"I can think of a place or two."

"I bet you can. And when I'm on duty it's my job to act as tour guide to all of those places, in return for some green attention."

"Green attention?"

"Long green attention. The attention everyone loves almost as much as sex. Moo-lah. Muh-knee."

Joe reached for his wallet. "Right."

Marlena laughed and grabbed his hand. "This is hypothetical, sweetie. I don't need money from *you*. I was just demonstrating the idea. You understand? It's all about attention. Wilderman said that money is nothing but attention. It used to be gold and silver, but now it's just an idea, just a matter of how we give attention to that idea."

"Who was Wilderman? Some kind of wise man?"

Guitar fanfare.

"Crazy man, more likely." Marlena shook her head and other parts vibrated in sympathy. "I just met him the once. That was enough, though."

"What was so crazy?"

"What wasn't? Guy was crazy, top to bottom. First of all, he was big. A really big guy. Short kind of spiky hair. Dark eyes that drew you in. Totally worked his assets, sort of like you. Except, I don't know, you're a natural. With him, it was something he did deliberately, switched it on and off at will. It's like he looked right into you and then gave you exactly what you needed."

"Hmmm... I wish I could do that."

"No, baby, you're perfect just the way you are."

"What did he do that was so crazy?"

Marlena stepped in close to Joe and he could feel the warmth radiating from her body. "You want me to tell you all about it? Tell you all the juicy details?"

"Um, sure," Joe said.

A subdued astral orchestra began to mask out the muttering jukebox, rising behind Marlena as she spoke.

"He came into the bar, right through that very door over there. He knew some of the regulars from way back, though I'm not sure how. He came and sat at the bar a few stools down from me. I was busy making a sale." She demonstrated her sales technique with a sidelong glance and a tilt of curvaceous hips.

"My customer wandered away for a moment and I was just sitting there, sipping my drink quietly, when I hear these sounds coming from this guy. Breathing. Like he was smoking a joint – only he didn't have a joint and when he did this breathing thing, I could feel it in my body. Right down there in the core of my being, shooting spasms of pleasure up my spine. Unbelievable. I swear I was having a full-tilt orgasm right there on my barstool, in just moments! And all he was doing was sitting there, ten feet away, making breathing noises with his mouth. Boom, baby!"

"No way," said Joe.

"I am a professional," Marlena said firmly. "I am fully qualified to identify an orgasm when I encounter one. And that was a damn fine one. He had my attention. So of course I went over to say hello. He went right to business."

"Business?"

"We worked out a deal, I ditched my customer and Wilderman and I went back to my room to perform the transaction."

"And how did that go?"

"It went on and on for hours and was really quite amazing, even though he did talk an awful lot. He was talking pretty much the whole time. I guess it had something to do with his side of the deal."

"What did he say?"

"I can only remember some of it. I was concentrating on, you know, professional technique, at the time. He talked a lot about how feelings could be colors or something like that and he told stories."

"He told stories? While you were, um, working?"

Marlena's voice got a little softer, more evenly spaced, and a lone astral violin began a Philip Glass theme of repeating triads. "Oh, yeah, he told a few stories and they seemed to connect up to what he was, you know, doing and with the other stuff he was saying about feelings and colors. It was impossible to tell if he was talking in a rhythm that followed our motion or if we were moving to the rhythm of his voice. Oh, yes. I was starting to feel really... different... warm and glowing... tingling... like we were totally connected and waves of energy flowed through us. Like we were really vast and connected to everything around us... Mmmm.... I only really remember one of the stories..."

"What was the story?"

"Let's see." She seemed to scan the ceiling for a moment. "It was fascinating, about a beautiful princess in a faraway land. She was a beautiful little white girl named Miranda who had the most perfect appearance. Miranda had thick, luxurious golden hair that reached all the way down her back. She had perky little titties and a nice round ass. Her legs were long and smooth and strong. Every day she would look in the mirror and marvel at the wonder of her own china-perfect face. She would put on her many different dresses and outfits and pose in front of the mirror. She would get butt-naked and watch her reflection twirl around. That reflection was so beautiful, she was such a lovely girl, that Miranda wanted to just look at her and be with her all day long. Looking was a bright warm tingle every time.

"After a long while, when Miranda had run out of dresses and poses, she started to imagine the mirror-girl doing different things, living a fantastic life out of view of reflective glass. Miranda's own life was not too bad, really. She was a princess and was always warm and well-fed, looked-after, in a lovely palace. But everyone else in the place was all about government and that was a subject that bored her to tears, literally and often. She didn't have much of a social life, except on rare, carefully planned Social Occasions. So she spent a lot of time with her mirror and got pretty skilled at thinking about what life was like on the other side of the glass.

"In Miranda's imagination, the mirror girl would show up excited and breathless, tingling and warm. She would tell Miranda of her exploits, stories set far away or sometimes just in the next room, with boys and girls and men and bandits and magicians and beggars and warriors and holy whores. Mmm, yes.

"One day the mirror girl showed up in a shimmering golden gown and told Miranda how she had been adopted by a clan of warriors with supernatural powers and made their queen. Another day she arrived flushed and barely dressed and told of her erotic adventure with a troupe of traveling acrobats. And on yet another occasion, she told Miranda of a secret order of women who welcomed her and showed her the mysteries of life.

"Miranda enjoyed these encounters with the mirror girl very much and for a long time. But eventually she began to feel unsatisfied. It wasn't fair that the mirror girl, who was exactly like her in every way, should be living the good life while Miranda returned again and again to her boring daily routine. The tingle had gone cold and turned around. In a moment of frustration, she said all this to the mirror girl. Instead of reflecting back her anger, as Miranda had expected, the mirror girl offered to help. The mirror girl proposed that Miranda would tell all about her life and then she would offer advice, suggestions about how Miranda might change things and make her life more wonderful and exciting.

"Miranda told the mirror girl all about her isolation. 'I just wish I could meet some new, interesting people,' she concluded.

"The mirror girl listened carefully to everything that Miranda said and then thought in silence for a few minutes. 'At midnight tonight,' the mirror girl said, 'climb out of your window and go into the town. Dress as a common girl.'

"So Miranda did as the mirror girl suggested. At first the town was strange and she felt alone, but after a while she found herself in a pub, dancing with boys and sipping with mild abandon from a glass of wine. She had a wonderful time and returned to her bedroom before anyone noticed, the tingle now glowing brightly.

"The next day Miranda sat before the mirror and told the mirror girl about her adventures just as the mirror girl told her own, somewhat more erotic adventure with a championship bicycle racing team. 'I never have any erotic adventures,' the princess complained. 'How can I have hot, spine tingling, butt clenching, toe curling… I mean, how can I have an erotic adventure?'

"The mirror girl thought for a bit and then said, 'At midnight tonight, dressed only in your most gossamer and revealing robe, go into the woods on the far side of the town.'

"So Miranda did as the mirror girl said and soon found herself wandering in the woods, a warm breeze caressing her nearly naked booty. In the woods she met a young man almost as nearly naked as she. 'I've come here every night for a year,' the young man said, 'and fantasized that I would meet a beautiful princess. And here you are.' Every night that they could both sneak out and meet they tingled for each other with great brilliance and heat.

"And so it went with Miranda and the mirror girl. Miranda would express her frustration in some area of her life and the mirror girl would tell her how to get what she wanted. Soon Miranda had tasted wonderful and exotic foods from all around the world. She wore the clothes of peasants, rogues, warriors and royalty. She gained power and influence over the people in her life and developed her own methods for getting things. She learned languages and science and philosophy. She had boys and girls, men and women to play with and she had times of joy, passion, ecstasy and awe. Warm bright tingling became the backdrop to every moment.

"One day she realized that she and the mirror girl shared equally in the tales of adventure. Miranda could go one for one and often surpass the mirror girl with stories of wildness and freedom and love and beauty. Once again, they were mirror images of each other. At that point, the mirror became a simple piece of reflecting glass again, the mirror girl just a reflection. Miranda went off to live her life. She married the naked boy from the woods, and eventually they became king and queen of the realm and ruled benevolently until, some years later, a major corporation paid them a lot of money to sell out the nation's mineral rights. Mm, hm. That's right."

10 ✶ A Catchy Name and a Dream

Marlena gestured to the bartender and a moment later two glasses of Old Mystery appeared. The hypnotic violin transformed into astral jazz and Marlena's voice picked up in volume and tempo. "That's the story I remember. There were a few others, but I don't remember them well enough to tell," she said.

"That was quite a bit to remember."

"Yes, the details came back to me as I told it. And the feelings…" She shuddered pleasurably, setting her goods and wares in motion. "I remember the feelings."

"So what happened then?" Joe asked. "With Wilderman." And an astral fanfare momentarily topped the jazz.

"Well, I'm not going to get into all that. I'd be talking all night when there are so many better things for us to be doing. Suffice it to say, he came across with his side of the deal, I paid him and he left."

"*You* paid *him*?"

"Oh, yes. I paid him a sizable amount of green attention, and I've been quite happy with what he gave me."

"What did he give you?"

Marlena leaned in close to him, her full lips near his ear. He could feel her breath against him, the warmth of her body close to his. She inhaled, as if preparing to say something significant – but instead just kept inhaling and exhaling through her mouth, almost as if she were smoking a joint. But there was no joint.

Joe felt a bolt of electricity enter him through the center of his chest – then shoot down his spine and into root of his cock, which immediately sprang to full attention. An astral rock guitar soared wildly to a triumphant climax and Joe grabbed the bar to steady himself. The only word he had to describe the sensation radiating from deep inside him was 'orgasm,' but it was different than any he had ever experienced. Instead of a spasm in his crotch, it started in his gonads and spread instantly through his entire body, exciting his nervous system as a whole. His hands tingled, his toes curled and his spinal column danced in waves. He was breathing like he just made the winning finish in a marathon race. Even though his cock was straining against his trousers, a compass needle seeking true pussy, he didn't squirt. Gasping, he clutched at the bar, panting, covered in a fine sweat as the feeling surged, whelmed, overwhelmed, and then faded.

"That's just a little sample," Marlena whispered in his ear. "You like?"

Joe grabbed a napkin from the bar and wiped his damp face.

"Heh heh," said Bob from down the bar. "Marlena give you one of her specials?"

"Damn," said Tim. "That's worth fifty bucks for sure."

"You should have her on your show." Bob gulped at his beer.

"Hell, you should have us on your show," Tim added.

Marlena grinned. "Why would Joe want your old, drunk, sorry asses on his show?"

"'Cause we know stuff," said Tim.

"Yeah," said Bob. "We know how it *is*."

Joe was starting to get his breath back. "What do you know?"

"He wants to know what we know," Tim chuckled.

"He has no idea what we know," Bob giggled.

"Guy like him knows a few things, too," observed Tim.

"Oh, yeah. He's a wise guy," Bob confirmed.

"Do you think he knows anything about marketing?"

"Must know something, television show and all."

Tim chuckled. "Think he knows how to gain rapport with a complete stranger – every time?"

"He got a freebie out of Marlena. And I kind of like him, too, in a purely friendly kind of way," Bob pointed out.

"Mirroring and matching," Tim said. "I've been watching. I can spot the moves of a pro."

"He's a natural," Bob said. "I liked him the moment I saw him."

"On TV?"

"Hmmm," said Bob. "No, just here, tonight, in person."

"So maybe he needs to know a thing or two about grabbing an audience on TV," Tim commented.

"What do you know about it?" Joe finally managed to squeeze a word in between Bob and Tim's interlocking thoughts.

"I tell you," Bob said, "we know stuff."

"Yeah," said Tim. "We *know* how it is."

The two old men laboriously climbed down from their stools and shuffled closer. Tim was tall and withered and Bob was shorter, plump and withered. Or maybe it was the other way around. They placed their drinks on the bar and gingerly hauled themselves onto a new set of stools before speaking again. An astral theme was wafting in, a solid rock'n'roll chord progression, the bass line just hinting at detective themes. It was presently mild, yet promising wildness to come and, Joe thought, a tiny bit incongruous with the old drunks who were presently holding forth.

"We're the best there is."

"At marketing and mind tech stuff."

"We're not as old as we look."

"But we've seen more than you'd believe."

"You have no idea what we've done."

"Why don't you tell me?" Joe suggested. "What's 'mind tech stuff'?"

"Most ad agencies just go with what they think looks good or sounds good or does well in testing."

"It's a kind of hit or miss thing."

"Which is why so many ads really suck."

"But some of us study the mind."

"And we know what really works."

The two old men tossed back their drinks and slid the empty glasses toward Joe, who signaled the bartender for refills. The Astral Score vamped for a few minutes until they had each taken a sip from a fresh drink.

"Mind tech's been around for decades," Bob continued.

"Everybody's poked their noses into it," added Tim.

"Governments of most nations, for military use and for domestic control."

"Corporations, for maximizing employee output and for increasing consumer demand."

"Religions, for imposing beliefs and restrictions."

"Schools, for learning and skill acquisition."

"Doctors, shrinks, hypnotists and all kinds of therapists, for healing and personal change"

"And then there are the crazies. Freelance social engineers."

"Culture jammers."

"Do-gooders and do-badders."

"Freakies who want to save the world."

"And freakers who want to end it."

"Always some damn hoo-ha to be had."

Bob and Tim sipped for a moment. "Hoo-ha?" Joe asked.

"A commotion, a row, a big whoopsie about whatever," Tim explained.

"The Rapture, Judgment Day, Ragnarok, the coming of the Space Brothers."

"The Jupiter Effect, Time Wave Zero, 2012."

"The Harmonic Convergence, The Eschaton, The Age of Aquarius."

"X-Day, Y2K, The Equinox of the Gods."

"The Great Purple Hoo-Ha?" Joe prompted.

Bob and Tim looked at each other, looked at Joe, gulped down the remnants of their drinks and then laughed until they coughed and gasped for air.

"That funny, huh?" Marlena commented.

"That's quite a funny turn of phrase," Tim said. "The Great Purple Hoo-Ha."

"And," Bob added. "It was our last job."

"I told you he knew a few things."

"Oh, I know he's a wise guy."

Joe tried to grasp what this meant as a rather pompous astral symphonic arrangement covered the pause in the conversation.

"Were you... cultists?" Joe finally asked. "Were you involved in that weird religion?"

"Cultists? Ha!" Bob scoffed.

"Ha!" added Tim. "We weren't any damn cultists."

"We work as mind tech specialists."

"That's what we do."

"So what are you doing here?" Joe queried.

"Yeah," said Marlena. "What the fuck? Mind tech specialists? You two old bastards?"

"You want to know about it?" Tim asked.

"Yeah," said Bob. "You want us to tell?"

"Sure," said Joe. "What do mind tech specialists do for whacked out end-of-the-world cultist weirdoes?"

They grinned at each other, slid their empty glasses toward Joe and waited expectantly. Joe nodded to the bartender and fresh booze was poured.

"You're a hell of a guy," Bob said.

"Yeah," said Tim. "A hell of guy."

They drank silently for a moment as the Astral Score cued a reprise of the rock and detective theme, playing it easy, building slowly. Finally, Bob and Tim set their glasses down, looked up and down the bar, and began to speak in hushed tones, as if they might be overheard.

"We were running our own consulting firm," Tim began.

"And we handled some serious accounts."

"We taught the world to think outside the box."

"Literally. I invented that phrase."

"And I sold it to, whatsisname, the guy who wrote the book."

"Now everyone has to think outside the box."

"We created the need for the Bed Breezer," Tim said.

"The simple tube that makes sleeping less stinky?" Joe asked. "They're one of our sponsors."

"That figures," said Bob.

"How did we ever live without that thing? Imagine! People farting under the blankets!" Joe was a little bit impressed.

"No one felt that way until after our campaign," Tim explained.

"That's right, most blankets floated six inches above the bed!"

"Or at least in our ads, they did."

"And we figured out the perfect way to catch and hold the attention of the common boob."

"The absolute perfect way to build suspense and get readers or listeners to keep on reading and listening, all the way through what you have to say."

"It was totally incredible."

"Worked every time."

"What was that?" Joe asked.

"We'll tell you soon."

"We had a storefront in the East Village," Bob said.

"It's all about information, doesn't matter where you are."

"Work globally, live locally."

"Only way to live."

"But sometimes we have to go onsite."

"Every once in while."

"Not very often at all."

"Just the once, really."

"Yeah, just the one time we went up to Poughkeepsie to meet the client."

"Who was that?" Joe interjected.

"The Great Purple Hoo-Ha," Bob chuckled.

"Incorporated," Tim added.

"The Great Purple Hoo-Ha, Incorporated?"

"What did you think it was called?" Bob asked.

"Whacked Out Nutballs, LLC?" Tim suggested.

"Might as well," said Joe. "So what was in Poughkeepsie?"

"Have you ever been to Poughkeepsie?" Tim asked.

"Heh heh," Bob said, nudging Tim with his elbow. "Has he ever been to Poughkeepsie?"

"Not that I recall," Joe said.

"You'd remember," said Bob.

"Or maybe you'd blank it out," Tim said.

"Everyone has a cough or a limp."

"And bad teeth. A cough, a limp, and bad teeth."

"It's not half as weird as Saugerties, though," Bob added, which made Tim laugh.

"Saugerties, heh. That's another story."

"The Hoo-Ha was in a big old warehouse down by the Hudson River. Noisy as hell."

"Really noisy. The Amtrak train would roar past about ten feet away, ten times a day."

"And it always seemed like there were fifteen things going on at once in there."

"Though we could only figure out a few of them."

"There were probably two hundred people in and out of there every day."

"Some of them were real weirdoes and freaks."

"Wore robes, tie-dyes, hippie-freaky-newagey types."

"But most of them were straight business types."

"Not quite suits."

"Suits who took risks."

"Suits that became a little frayed around the edges, fringe types."

"Nice metaphor, Bob."

"Thanks, Tim."

"They were there for the money."

"The money was good."

"Or they were there because of the work."

"Totally cutting edge stuff."

"An obscure religious cult in Poughkeepsie? Cutting edge?" Joe was working hard to put it together and the Astral Score wasn't helping any. The more Bob and Tim spoke, the more mysterious the music became, detective themes building on ska roots with horns and scat vocals.

"Our first day there we saw rooms full of people hard at it," Tim explained.

"The Internet Department," Bob continued. "The Direct Marketing Department. The Book Publishing Division. Pamphlets and Cards."

"Press Relations. Group Dynamics. Seminars and Workshops."

"Media of every type."

"Publishing, broadcasting, dissemination."

"Which all sounds about right," Bob commented.

"Until you start to examine the information flowing through that media," Tim explained.

"What was it?" Joe asked.

Bob: "Monitoring and implementation."

Tim: "Collecting media from millions of sources worldwide."

"Mining it, collating it."

"Watching for trends."

"Watching for new memes."

"Watching for new entities."

Joe was still confused. "For what purpose?"

"The media landscape, the noosphere, if you will, is like a big puzzle."

"If you want to add something to it, it has to fit with what's already there."

"Like a key in a lock."

"Like a customer in Marlena's –"

"In the palm of her hand. Heh heh."

"And even more, if you can find a big entity rising…"

"A new school of thought or art. A new way of thinking."

"A new industry or new media."

"If you can find a big flow of attention running in one direction…"

"You can use it. Ride on it. Surf it."

"And if you're really good…"

"You can make it your own."

"That's what the, uh, G.P.H.H. is trying to do?" Joe asked.

"That's what they're doing."

"Oh, yeah. That's what they're doing."

The old men were momentarily quiet and the Astral Score subdued. Bob and Tim looked down at their empty glasses and then slid them toward Joe, who ordered refills all around.

When lips were once again moistened, Joe prompted them on. "So The Great Purple Hoo-Ha is one of these entity things? And you were hired to ride it? Or co-opt it?"

"The G.P.H.H., Inc. is the Founder and his employees, disciples, whatever you want to call them."

"But the Great Purple Hoo-Ha itself. We don't know what the hell that really is."

"It wasn't very far along when we were there."

"We were working on a precursor."

"I don't think the Founder had much of an idea then, either."

"Just a catchy name and a dream."

"We were working on Project Opener."

"We were developing an entity that could open the way for other entities."

"An entity that operated within its own paradigm of reality."

"Its own epistemology that would allow it to communicate with other entities."

"Help or hinder them. Teach them how to rise into the media landscape."

"How to emerge into the noosphere as major players."

"And it would teach its own paradigm, its own way of thinking."

"And anyone it taught could perceive entities and call them forth."

"Then the Opener entity could teach the Founder."

"And the Founder could bring forth an enormous entity..."

"A Great Purple Hoo-Ha."

"But we never got as far as all that."

Joe laughed. "I'm not surprised. It sounds like bullshit to me."

"Well, thank you for saying so," Bob offered.

"We've spent a lot of time studying this stuff," Tim added.

"I don't buy any of this entity crap," Joe continued. "You don't just decide to create the fucking end of the world, do some demographics and market analysis and poof! Some entity thing pops out and ushers in the, uh, The Equinox of the Gods, whatever the hell that is."

"You're absolutely right, Joe." Tim said.

"Yeah, it's not all that simple," Bob elaborated.

"Takes a lot more than demographics and analysis."

"That's for sure."

"So none of this ever happened, right?" Joe asked. "There never was an Opener and there never can be a Great Purple Hoo-Ha, whatever that's supposed to be?"

"Oh, no," said Bob. "We created the Opener just fine."

"Maybe a little too fine," said Tim.

"There's a point where these things are supposed to take on a life of their own."

"But usually that's just a metaphor."

"This thing – well –"

"It's alive."

Joe scoffed. "What?"

"Oh yeah. It slipped our control almost immediately."

"We spent a lot of time trying to track it."

"And so did a lot of other people."

"The government was on its tail."

"Some heavy spook types showed up, snooping around."

"Things got kind of tense."

"Not our idea of a healthy work environment."

"And the Opener, well –"

"– it does some weird shit."

"Weird shit?"

"Yeah," said Bob. "It was created to have a unique ability to communicate with and influence other entities."

"That's right," added Tim, "and humans are entities, too."

"Has some weird effects on humans."

"It can teach us and it can - change us."

"It makes changes directly to the neurology. Subtle, tiny changes."

"But it only takes subtle changes in your brain to change your whole life."

"We saw some stuff."

"We saw people turn into complete degenerates."

"We saw people completely forget who they were."

"We saw a man who wore pink tutus."

"We saw a woman who talked to her lunch."

"We saw a Chinese guy who thought he was Vanilla Ice."

"We saw a couple people who just lost their minds."

"Batshit crazy."

"We saw one person lose her life."

"Finally we got the hell out of there."

"But not without paying a price," Tim said.

They both got very quiet and the tempo of their astral theme slowed down almost to nothing.

"We sure paid a price," Bob said.

"Penalties for breaking your contract?" Joe asked.

"You could say that."

"How much?"

"Forty-five," said Bob

"Forty-five?" Joe repeated.

"Forty-five years," said Tim.

"How old do you think we are?" Bob demanded.

"I don't know," said Joe. "Eighty-five?"

"I'm thirty-nine," said Tim.

"I'm thirty-seven," said Bob. "I was thirty-one when we took the job."

Marlena laughed. "I've heard this shit before. They try this on every woman who walks in the door. Thirty-seven my round, brown ass. You wrinkly old bastards probably can't even remember when you were thirty-seven. If you're thirty-seven, I'm a virginal sixteen!"

Tim, or maybe it was Bob – the short, fat one, at any rate – climbed down from his stool and wobbled unsteadily over to Marlena. He looked her up and down with an appraising eye. "If I were…If I…" he coughed. "Oh, fuck," he said, shaking his head, and wobbled back to his stool. He gulped whatever drops of booze remained in his glass and fell silent.

"You're telling me that they made you old?" Joe asked.

"Something sure as fuck did," said Bob.

Tim remained silent.

"Do you have any proof of this?"

Tim kept his silence, but produced his wallet and displayed a driver's license. Joe took a look: Timothy X. Arley of New York City, born thirty-nine years previously. A picture of a plump-faced white guy, approaching middle age.

Marlena gave it a cursory glance and snorted. "I know the guy up the block who prints these things. Mostly fake I.D.s for illegals and minors, but he'll print up pretty much anything, if you pay him."

"If you don't believe," Bob said, "why not ask the spook?"

"Ask who?" Joe inquired.

"Heh heh," said Tim, finally. "Yeah, ask the spook."

"Excuse me," asserted Marlena. "The spook?"

"We told you. The government spied on the whole thing."

"We were shown pictures."

"So we'd know who they were and wouldn't be fooled into, you know, spilling the beans."

"So we recognized her when we saw her hanging around the cafeteria."

"And she's still on the job."

"Spook lady over there's been in here almost every night for months." Bob gestured not very discretely toward a booth at the far end of the room, occupied by a woman in a dark suit. She was having a conversation with a Hispanic man in a flowered shirt and she occasionally glanced toward the bar.

"Sometimes she's with another spook lady."

"Sometimes she's alone."

"They must think we're still in the game."

"Who cares? She can watch what we do here."

"We're just here for the drinks."

"She was one of the ones, back then."

"Spying on Project Opener."

As they were speaking, the woman and the Hispanic man ended their conversation. The man wandered off and the woman turned to look frankly at the group gathered at the bar.

"Woh," said Tim. "She's on to us."

"Go on," Bob said to Joe. "Go ask her about us."

"She needs to know we're on to her, too."

"Then maybe she'll go away."

"Why don't you talk to her?" Joe queried.

"Look at us," Tim said. "We can't do much."

"Not like you, Joe. You're the only one here who can do it."

"You may not believe us, but we believe in you."

"We admire you."

"Maybe she saw your friend, Joe," Marlena suggested.

"Yeah, yeah. Go talk to her." Bob urged Joe on, waving his arms in a feeble, drunken way, as if he were trying to direct traffic.

11 ✱ Project Woohoo

The astral detective theme rose fully to the surface, now emphasizing orchestral tension and drama as Joe stood and navigated toward the woman in the booth. She watched him unabashedly. She wore a soot-black man's suit and her matching black hair was chopped short just below her ears. She appeared to be in her mid-thirties and seemed athletic and lean under the not-quite-government issue attire.

She smiled broadly as Joe approached. "Say, aren't you that guy from TV?"

"Yeah," Joe said. "Show, Schmoe, whatever. Shove it up your ass."

"Wow, it's really nice to meet you, too," the woman grinned. "We don't get many celebrities in this dive."

"I'm not much of a celebrity," Joe said, sliding into the booth across from her. "I'm fit for a dive."

"Oh, come now," she said. "Look at you! You're quite a celebrity!"

"Sure, whatever," Joe said. "Were you here in the bar last night?"

"Sure," she said. "Sitting right here in this booth."

"Do you remember who I was talking to?"

"What? You mean last night?"

"Right, last night. I was sitting right over there, talking to someone. Did you see him?"

"You were here in the bar last night? I think I would have remembered that."

"Yeah, yeah, right, right. Next subject: My acquaintances over there by the bar think you're some kind of, er, spook."

She looked over at the bar, where Bob, Tim, Marlena and the bartender were working hard to look nonchalant, then back at Joe. "What gave them that idea?"

"Oh, I don't know," said Joe. "Maybe it's the shoes."

She looked down at her shiny black shoes. Then suddenly she laughed a deep, truncated guffaw. "Right," she said. "The shoes."

"So you are a spy?"

"*Former* spy, please," she said. "And please call me Judy, Mr. Schmoe."

"Fuck you, Judy," said Joe. "For dog's sake, please, call me Joe."

"I feel like we're old friends, Joe. Like I can trust you. And I don't trust anyone. That's odd."

"Uh, right," said Joe. "Anyway, the two old geezers at the bar say you know them and you can tell me their real age."

"Do I know them? Can't say I do... I mean, I'm in here a lot. I've seen them in here... and... did you say, 'their real age'?"

"Yes, they claim to be somewhat younger than they look."

Judy stared hard at Bob and Tim for a moment and a hint of Theremin mixed in with the orchestral arrangement. Her eyes grew wide. "Is it them?" The Theremin grew louder. "Holy crap! It is them! One of the Anomalies. Bob and, uh, Jim."

"Tim."

"Right, Tim! That's so incredible. Did they tell you what happened to them?"

"That they got old, yes. So you're saying it's true?"

"Yes, yes, it's true! And that wasn't the strangest thing... I... am not at liberty to share this information even with you, Joe."

"Oh, come on, Judy. Don't you trust me?"

She looked confused for a moment and then grinned sheepishly. "Well, I suppose it's okay, since it's you, Joe."

"You were there, in Poughkeepsie?"

"Oh, yes. Your old men there were hired geeks. At the time, both appeared to be in their late thirties. Then one day we tuned in and they were old. They didn't stick around much after that."

"You were spying on them?"

"On Bob and Jim?" Judy laughed. "Small time. There were bigger things going on in Po-town."

"The Great Purple Hoo-Ha?"

"A front for forces that intend to destabilize our government and economy."

"I thought they were a bunch of religious whackos"

"It's common for these, um, significant forces to encourage whackos when it suits their ends. Hitler's people encouraged a whacko Bolshevik to burn the Reichstag Building so they could blame it on Bolsheviks, for instance, and consolidate their power on that basis. In this case, though, we suspect that the entire organization was co-opted by something very, very powerful. It became headquarters for a jihad of psychological warfare. Culture jamming on an order never seen before."

The Astral Score had been growing more symphonic and was now tilting toward ominous kettle drums and deep-hooting horns. "What made you suspect it was a front?" Joe asked.

"Why else would someone go to all that trouble, if not to operate on a global scale? They are aiming for something really big. Something at the top of the list: overthrow the government."

"Or take over the world," Joe suggested.

"You'd have to overthrow a lot of governments."

"So if you weren't spying on Project Opener…"

"Project Opener," Judy asked, "what's that?"

"What Bob and Jim over there were working on, or so they say."

"Oh, okay. That. A clever marketing project. Memetics. Nice stuff, but nothing unusual."

"So what were you spying on?"

"We were observing Project Woohoo," she said, "which had much greater ramifications."

"Woohoo?"

"Yes."

"What exactly was Project Woohoo?"

"We're still not sure; I can only tell you what I saw. People who were instantly and completely indoctrinated into the cult's degenerate lifestyle. People who experienced complete amnesia and were susceptible to personality replacement."

"Personality replacement?"

"Yes, it's how you create moles and sleeper agents, Manchurian candidates and mindless followers. Among other things. And we did see some examples of complete personality replacement. For instance, there was a Chinese guy who was replaced with a gangsta rapper. Weird and deeply disturbing stuff, Joe. Imagine if world leaders were kidnapped and their personalities replaced with those of terrorists or ideologues!"

"Then they'd act just as batshit crazy as they always do," Joe said. "Most world leaders are already terrorists and ideologues."

"Exactly!" Judy exclaimed. "Maybe it's already happened! If something is possible, then someone out there is insane enough to do it."

"Hmmm," said Joe. "That might explain the Vice President…"

Judy looked up sharply. "How did you know about the Vice President?"

Joe laughed nervously. "Know? I just… I mean… Really?"

"It's a theory," Judy said.

"So what else did you see?" Joe asked.

"Enough people who flipped their lids to fill a medium-sized looney-bin. And there was a death, a young woman who was at the center of the whole project. They were experimenting on her, she was the subject. God knows what they were trying to do or exactly how she died. They worked hard to cover the whole thing up. Made up a story. When it hit the news it wasn't a human guinea pig who had been murdered, it was a dead hooker who had O.D.ed in the Founder's apartment. It was a big scandal and the Founder was charged with manslaughter and acquitted. All a big show and it drew attention away from what really was going on, from Project Woohoo. But that wasn't the weirdest thing. The weirdest thing…"

"Yes?"

"The food in the cafeteria…"

"Yes?"

"One day my lunch spoke to me."

"Say what?"

She unbuttoned her suit jacket, revealing the front of a crisp white shirt, and leaned back. She took a sip from her drink and sighed. "I've never told this to anyone," she said.

"Go on," Joe suggested.

"There was some old man who was bothering me, an old black guy with a cane who kept trying to talk to me, saying something about deception or some such. At first I thought maybe my cover was blown, but then I remembered seeing him around. He was a janitor or something and he was trying to witness to me."

"Witness?"

"Yes, sir. Like a born-again Christian, or a Jehovah's Witness. But I told him to keep on moving. And he said something odd. He said, 'If you won't listen to me, then the next entity you encounter will tell you.'"

"Fuck," said Joe. "More entities."

"Yes," said Judy. "They talk like that in Poughkeepsie. Anyway, the old guy finally wanders off and I start to unwrap my lunch. All the cafeteria food there is covered in plastic shrink wrap. I was having a difficult time unwrapping the plate. Hell, I couldn't even really tell what was in it. I was tugging at it, and I could feel something on the plate go squish – like my dessert was now mush or something – and I cursed at the plate." She paused.

"Right," Joe said. "You cursed at it."

"Yes, sir. I said, 'Come on, you son of a bitch.' And the plate of food said, 'Dog meat is not approved by the Dutchess County Department of Health and you will find only chicken here. No bitches or sons of bitches have been harmed in the making of this lunch.'

"Needless to say, I was surprised. I've never had a talking chicken salad sandwich before. The plastic suddenly came off, then, very easily – but my appetite was gone. I just stared and maybe stuttered a little."

"Perhaps the food was drugged?" Joe suggested.

"I hadn't eaten the damn food yet. But, yes, there is the possibility that someone or something in that place had covertly drugged me. Damn odd drug, though, if so. Other than the talking food, everything else was very normal."

"So what did the chicken salad sandwich say?"

"It said, 'You remind me of the guy at the Endless Feast.'

"'This is no endless feast,' I responded, 'just lunch.'

The Astral Score became quiet, increasingly atmospheric, waves of sound rising and falling in the background.

"The sandwich laughed a little bit and so did the apple cobbler, I think, even though it was kind of flat. 'The Endless Feast was lunch, twenty four hours a day and always the same,' the chicken salad on toast explained. 'On the table in front of the man was an ornate china plate that was always piled high with roast beef sandwiches, deep-fried onion rings, and cole slaw. The food was delicious and he would eat it whenever he got hungry. Meal after meal of wonderful roast beef sandwiches, onion rings, and slaw. How could life be any better?'

"'A cold drink?' I suggested.

"'Well, of course he had a cold drink,' the sandwich said. 'Of course! Always a cold drink! Milk, actually, that's what the guy liked, cold, frosty milk. Every day, every meal, with every roast beef sandwich: ice-cold milk. And it was heavenly. Everything was provided for and life was an Endless Feast.

"'And then one day, someone else came along and sat down at the table, about fifteen feet away from the man. This other man sat down and started eating something that was very clearly *not* a roast beef sandwich.'

"'What was it?' I asked.

"'Pate de fois gras, on a Schnitz cracker,' the chicken salad sandwich explained. '"What is that?" the man cried out.

"''"Goose liver," said the other man. "There's plenty of it down here." He pointed to the table, which stretched off into the distance, laden with food of every sort. "And it is yummy. Oh yes." And the other man wandered off.

"'The man sat there for quite a while, unsure what to do. He had never really noticed how long the table actually was, or that it was laden with so much variety of food. Why look past the tasty roast beef sandwiches? But… goose liver? That sounded entirely unappetizing. So roast beef it was, for yet another meal.

"'But then, a little while later, a young woman appeared at the table, about twenty five feet away, and started eating something that was neither roast beef sandwiches or pate de fois gras on a Schnitz. "What is that?" the man called.

"''"Gorgonzola cheese," the woman said, her mouth full and chewing. "And it is really, really good. Here! Taste a bit!" And she marched down to the man and held out a large chunk of fragrant cheese. She smiled warmly as he took the cheese between his fingers and tentatively lifted it to his face. He smelled it and it was funky but intriguing. He bit off a tiny bit and chewed. And was suddenly overcome by the rich flavor. It was a totally different flavor, not roast beef, not onion ring, not cole slaw. Something else entirely and… it was good! He greedily devoured the rest of the cheese. He looked up to find the young woman gawking at him in mild amazement. As their eyes met, they started to laugh. "Thank you!" the man called, but the young woman had already turned and begun to walk away.

"'The man sat there for a long while, unsure and a bit overwhelmed. Then, suddenly, the decision blazed upon his consciousness: He would have more cheese! And young women! So finally he stood and started to take a step and *clank*! Heavy, black iron chains held him back. He was dimly aware that chains had been present his whole life; sometimes he wondered what they were for. Now he knew.

"He struggled against the chains. He fought and pulled and writhed. He banged the chains against the chair and against the floor. The clatter attracted the occasional notice of a passing diner – who would decide to avoid the situation in favor of better fare – but the chains still held, iron bands snugly gripping his arms and legs.

"'Finally he grew tired of the struggle and sat quietly again. He munched a roast beef sandwich and allowed his mind to calm down. When he was once again calm and well-fed, he took stock of his situation. He looked at the food on the table. He looked at the chains. Really looked at them, for the first time, and saw just how snugly they held his arms and legs. And he noticed that his arms and legs, much like the rest of him, were, to be polite, quite chubby. Of course! He had devoured beef sandwiches and deep fried onion rings for decades, at best count, without much exercise.

"'He thought about it and decided that it just might work. He'd have to give up something he loved – just for a while – to find all the possibilities that he could love. He'd have to go on a diet until he lost enough body blubber to slip out of his manacles!'

"The chicken salad sandwich fell silent. 'So did he do it?" I asked. 'Did the man escape his chains?'

"'After a couple false starts and a few agonizing months of semi-starvation, yes, he finally did.'

"'What happened? Was he happy? Did he find the young woman?'

"'I couldn't tell you,' the chicken salad sandwich said. 'Once he slipped his bonds, he walked right out of the story. Maybe to another part of the Endless Feast table, or perhaps he wandered away from the table altogether and found some other opportunities. That's the end of the story. You can eat me now.'"

"So did you?" asked Joe.

Judy shook her head. "Did I what?"

"Did you eat the sandwich?"

"Hell no. I tossed the tray into the trash and got the fuck out of there. Checked myself in for psych eval. I retired shortly after."

"That's a fascinating story," Joe said.

"Well, that's what it was like in Poughkeepsie," Judy said. "But that's not why you should have me on your show."

"And why should I have you on my show?"

The Astral Score had been momentarily silent. Now, suddenly, it rocked as Judy grabbed the front of her crisp white shirt and tore it open, buttons popping and ricocheting off the table. She arched her back to show off her breasts, round, bobbing melons caught in the filmy, sheer fabric of her bra.

"You're on," Joe said.

The Great Purple Hoo-Ha

12 ✱ The Next Day

There was a click, the background hum changed tone slightly, and Joe could hear the phone at the other end start to ring, a little electronic cricket in his ear. The number had been easy to obtain – Joe knew people whose job description was essentially tracking down celebrities. Even celebrities who had disappeared from the social landscape for a few years.

Joe thought about what he would say, what he could say that wouldn't set off a medium-sensitive bullshit detector. What if Adam had lied? Joe would really sound nuts.

Another ring and then "Hello?" It was just a simple hello, but the voice was so full of phlegm, scratchy and goopy at the same time, it made Joe recoil from the phone. Just slightly, and just for a moment. The Astral Score played a sour chord on a hellish electric guitar.

"Hello," said Joe, using his on-air voice. "This is Joe Maloney, from Joe's Show. Am I speaking to Rex Massenclear?"

"Yeah," the voice oozed. "What do you want?"

"I think we have a mutual acquaintance," Joe said. "Adam?"

"Adam? What the fuck are you talking about?"

"You don't know Adam? Young guy, kind of wild hair? I need to talk to you, Rex, about Adam."

"I don't know your friend Adam. I don't know what your game is," Rex said, "but you can just fuck right off." There was a click and even the Astral Score was silent.

He didn't seem all that disgusting, Joe thought.

The Great Purple Hoo-Ha

13 ✷ The Sex Lives of Spies

The camera pulled in tight on Joe. He glanced at the monitor. Yeah, he looked good. Totally ready. Totally feeling good. His theme music faded, but the Astral Score continued the melody on a lone acoustic guitar.

"Our government spends untold billions of dollars every year on spying activities. That means that there are a lot of spies out there. Not all of them are spying on other countries. Some agencies have license to spy within our own borders. Is that a good thing? How else would the government combat terrorist cells and other conspiratorial threats? Perhaps it takes a spy to stop a spy. Is it a bad thing? I don't know about you, but I'd rather not have someone spying on me. Not that I have anything to hide…" He laughed.

"Now don't worry, my friends," Joe continued as the camera pulled out. "We're not about to do an expose on government spending and we're not about to go moral on you here in any way. Come on, people, you watched those old James Bond movies, too… 007 saw plenty of hot undercover action. Don't you wonder about the sex lives of real spies?"

The audience cheered and hooted.

"Tonight on Joe's Show: The Sex Lives of Spies! Or, at least, that's how we're going to get this party started. Who knows where we may end up before the hour is over? Are you ready?"

More cheering and hooting. The audience had cue cards, too.

"Ladies, gentlemen, and this person over here, too, please welcome Betty and Judy, our two spies." The lights came up on the set, revealing two women dressed as Men in Black, seated on a long sofa: Judy with dark, cropped hair, and Betty with blond. They wore dark shades and exuded an aura of danger and mystery. Perfect, Joe thought.

Joe wandered over and skooched in next to Judy. After an exaggerated moment of making himself comfortable, he turned toward the women. "Judy and Betty here are former operatives for an agency that we will not name. Ladies, what kind of work were you engaged in?"

"Mostly work related to homeland security," Betty explained. "We kept tabs on domestic organizations that could potentially pose a threat to our nation and our people."

"Kept tabs?" Joe prompted. "How did you do that?"

"Observation," said Judy, "and infiltration."

"So that means that you pretended to join these groups and gained the trust of and socialized with terrorists and others?"

"Mostly others," said Judy. "But, yes."

Joe leaned in a little and the Astral Score paused for a beat. "So what was the sex like?"

The Hoot card was shown to the audience.

"Hot," Judy said.

"Yeah, very hot," said Betty.

More hooting.

Judy unbuttoned her suit jacket and leaned back in her seat, offering just a hint that she might not actually be a *Man* in Black.

"What are we talking about here?" Joe asked. "Straight sex with terrorist men? Lesbian sex with fellow operatives? What?"

The two spies looked at each other and smiled a little. "Oh, there was all of that," said Betty. "And more. Much more. Some of the groups we infiltrated were, um, culturally deviant. They had some odd customs."

"What were some of the unusual customs you encountered?"

"Uncomfortable underwear," said Betty, shifting in her seat.

"Social nudity," added Judy.

"Total female submission," Betty cooed.

"Total male submission," Judy grinned.

"Sex lotteries."

"Sexual yoga."

"Sexual magick."

"Whoa! Whoa!" Joe exclaimed. "Let's take them one at a time. Uncomfortable underwear?"

Betty leaned forward. "That's right. For penance, among other reasons. Kind of a masochistic thing. And also as something that everyone in the group would have in common. If you met another member of your group or cell, well, you knew that their privates itched just as much as yours. It's a kind of bonding, I think."

"Okay," said Joe. "How about social nudity?"

"There's much less of that than you'd think," Judy explained. "But we certainly encountered it. In some culturally deviant organizations, there just isn't the kind of body taboo we have in mainstream culture. And in some groups, they still feel the taboo, but getting naked together is their way of punching through the consensus culture, if you know what I mean. It's a reaction or a rebellion. Either way, it's quite liberating... er, I mean deviant."

Hoot!

"Okay," Joe said. "Betty, what did you mean by 'total female submission'?"

"Oh, that's old school terrorism, where the ideology is derived from patriarchal religious traditions. The Koran, for instance, or The Bible. Essentially, the women do everything the men tell them to do."

"Everything?" Joe insinuated.

Betty smiled mysteriously. "Everything."

Hoot! Hoot!

"Isn't that sometimes degrading and disgusting?"

Betty's smile widened and she nodded. "Mm hmm."

Joe shook his head. "Okay, Judy, what did you mean by 'total male submission'?"

"Well, sometimes the ideology is more matriarchal and the men are just obedient little puppy dogs who want to fulfill our every whim." Judy squirmed a little in her seat.

"Every whim?" Joe inquired.

Judy grinned. "*Every* whim."

Hoot! Hoot! Woooo!

"All right, now. Sex lotteries? What's a sex lottery?"

"In some of the more, um, goal-oriented terrorist organizations," Betty explained, "they believe that relationships and romantic attachments are hindrances on missions where you might have to abandon a comrade or even help one be martyred. On the other hand, they do recognize that humans complain a lot less when they have regular, even frequent sexual outlet. So, everyone's name goes into a hat..."

"And you have to have sex with whoever picks you?"

"You do your best to please," Betty said.

Hooooot!

"Okay, okay," Joe crowed. "Tell us about sexual yoga. What's that?"

"It's part of a yoga tradition called Tantra," Judy began, "and it involves maintaining a position for long periods of time, sometimes for hours…"

"A sexual position?" Joe asked. "Not necessarily a yoga position?"

"Both," said Judy. "There are special sex positions for Tantra. Not all that difficult really. Um, kind of fun, actually. And… and…"

"Yes?"

"The orgasms…"

"Yes?"

"Sometimes they can last for hours, too."

Hoooooot! Hoooooot!

"Wow!" Joe exclaimed. "Other than fantastic orgasms, is there a reason that a terrorist group would do this?"

"I don't think any of the Tantric groups we met were actively terrorists," said Judy. "But it was fun finding out they weren't. Like the other culturally deviant activities we've been talking about, there is religious ideology at the root of this. It's sort of like prayer, you know. Although with any activity like this, something can always go wrong."

"Such as?"

"We met one Tantric guru – you might know who I'm talking about; it made the news – who was obviously in it just for the sex. That's all he did, day and night. His followers thought he was just so spiritual, you know. I think the medical term is 'priapism.' His lever was stuck in the 'on' position, so he made it his career. While he was up to his neck in young, spiritual pussy, his chief of operations took over the organization and then actually took over a couple of towns, out west. We had to take them down."

"Right, then," said Joe. "Betty, you mentioned something else."

"Sexual magick?" Betty offered.

"That's right. Is that something different than sexual yoga?"

"Well, we like to combine," Betty began, than paused. "I mean, some of these culturally deviant organizations like to combine the sexual yoga and magick, though I suppose they don't strictly have to be combined."

"What's the difference?" Joe prompted.

"Sexual magick is, um, more goal-oriented," Betty explained. "You take all this sexual energy and aim it toward an objective. You make something happen. There are groups that spend their time aiming their sex magick at specific changes in the culture at large."

"So you actually did this?"

"That's right." Betty nodded.

"What was the aim of your sex magick?"

"I'm not at liberty to discuss that, Joe."

"Okay. But can you tell us – did it work?"

Betty smiled a little. "Yes."

"Okay, then," Joe read on. "Ladies, please tell me, you were spending your time with these groups and engaging in all of these wonderfully, er, deviant activities – just what made you do it?"

"Well, you know," Betty said, "You're there, there's not much else to do."

"What would you do, Joe?" Judy asked.

"Oh, ho ho, I'm not going to touch that one," Joe chuckled. "Let's see if the audience has any questions for you." He stood and strode down into the audience.

A big man in the third row stood up and Joe made his way over. "Do you have a question for the spies?" Joe asked.

"Yeah," said the man. "So far this is a lot of talk. You look like cops in cheap suits. Nothing sexy about you."

Audience: Wooooooooooooo!

"Ladies," Joe said, "are you ready to show them what it means to be a spy?"

"You bet, Joe," Judy and Betty said together, standing and removing their shades. On the set's sound system, a honky-tonk piano began to play and an astral orchestra swelled along with it. The spies strode confidently to the front of the stage and posed for a dramatic moment, tugging the fronts of their not-quite-government-issue shirts. A sudden loud rip and the cameras pulled in on big round breasts bobbing in the skimpiest of bikini tops. The spies posed and flirted with the cameras.

The audience was hooting even before they could see the card.

From somewhere just offstage, Joe could hear Jerry Hull exclaim, "Now *that's* good television!"

84 ✷ **The Great Purple Hoo-Ha**

14 ✶ Proof

After a short commercial break, Betty and Judy were settled on the long couch while Joe paced dramatically closer to the front of the stage. The two remarkably fit and athletic spies had stripped down to bikini tops and hot pants and the cameramen were doing their best to include them in nearly every shot.

"If you tuned in last week," Joe said, "you might remember that we had as our guest a woman whose daughter had joined a strange cult. These cultists not only capture the minds of young people, they believe in the coming of a day or event or entity – their version of Armageddon - that they call The Great Purple Hoo-Ha." Joe paused in case there was a laugh, but there was only a smattering of snickers.

"The GPHH cult, if we may call it that, turns out to be somewhat more worrisome than we had first considered. Our friends here, the lovely Judy and Betty, have some inside information that might be important. Ladies? Can you tell us what you know about this weird end-of-the-world cult?"

Betty smiled for the camera and leaned forward a little. "The GPHH was our final assignment before we retired from active spying," she began. "We lived and worked with these people for over three months and I've got to say, it was… it was…" She explored a series of facial expressions and then finally said, "very creepy."

A familiar B-movie sci-fi theme was astrally audible.

"Creepy?" Joe pursued. "How so?"

"Everything about it," Betty continued. "Their overall goal, I think, is to disrupt our entire way of life… It is both deviant and subversive in the extreme… and the way they intend to do it…"

"How do they intend to do it?"

Judy spoke up. "Mind control. And… I'm not sure how to say this, but I'll just go ahead and blurt it out, even though it probably is still classified: weird occult powers. We were talking about sex magick earlier – these guys are the champs."

"What can they do with their weird powers?" Joe asked.

"Sometimes it's big and dramatic – like when they need money or vehicles or something, it always turns up, right on time," Betty explained. "But mostly it's subtle stuff, a shift in someone's personality, a decision weighted just a little more in one direction, a coincidence that changes travel plans or delivery times or something like that."

"That doesn't sound very powerful," Joe observed.

"Applied at just the right place and time," Judy said, "any one of those things could change the course of history. If Hitler woke up in a good mood, or suffered from gastric reflux disorder at a crucial moment in the war, World War Two might have ended years earlier, or continued on years longer. Tough to predict – but if you get it right…"

"Okay," said Joe. "I get it and gastric reflux disorder can be pretty scary. Tell us about mind control."

"From what we observed," Betty began, "the founder of the GPHH has the ability to covertly hypnotize and plant suggestions in just about anyone. He can make someone laugh or yawn or fart or cream their shorts, at his unspoken signal."

There was a brief astral fanfare played on electric guitar.

"That's freaky," said Joe. "And just a little bit unbelievable."

"But even worse," continued Judy, "is what they do with new recruits. They make them practice a series of exercises that seem harmless enough. Kind of silly, really. Games where you lift people up and down or make mental images of friends. But over the course of time, even just a few days, the exercises subtly start to change your mind. It programs you for sex magick, gives you the, um, attitude to make it work. Makes you crave it."

"Makes you crave sex?" Joe asked.

"Makes you crave *sex magick*," Judy clarified.

Joe turned to face the audience and the camera pulled in on his face. "Friends, do you believe this stuff? Isn't this all a bit too far out to be real?"

Hoots, cheering, and scattered wolf whistles.

"Do you think we need more proof?"

Hoots, cheers, stomping.

"Perhaps we can do something about that." Joe paced across the set. "Ladies and gentlemen, yes, and you over here, we have with us a spokesperson for the Hoo-Ha cult." He paused to allow a bit of giggling. "And also Esty Westheimer, the daughter of Mrs. Westheimer, our guest last week who told us how her daughter was snatched away by the GPHH."

Two people emerged from stage right and came down onto the set. Joe intercepted them and briefly shook hands with each. One was a man in his mid-thirties, short dark hair, clean cut, wearing a Hawaiian shirt with gold pineapples on it and a pair of khaki pants. The other – Joe's heart had skipped a beat when he met her backstage earlier and it did the same now, with cameras rolling - the other was Esty, slim, black curly hair, delicate features, in clean black jeans and a tight sweater. She was quiet, seemed thoughtful, and was well-spoken and confident when she did speak.

The two joined Betty and Judy on the long couch. The man sat closest to Joe, with Esty just beyond.

"Okay," Joe began. "This is Damon Dark, from Great Purple Hoo-Ha, Incorporated. I have that right?" The man nodded. "And seated next to him is Esty Westheimer, who we heard all about last week, when her mother came on the show. Let me direct the first question to you, Mr. Dark."

"Yes?"

"Damon Dark. How did you come by an unusual name like that?"

"My parents were Dark."

"Ah," said Joe, "so you mean it's not a weird cult name or something like that."

"No, it's my real name and Great Purple Hoo-Ha, Incorporated is not a cult," Dark said. "We're a society of free individuals on a common mission."

"Well okay, then, Mr. Dark." He paused to look dramatically at the audience. The expression of mystery on his face was aided by the weeping of the astral Theremin. "Can you please tell us? What is your mission?"

"It's not an easy thing to define," Dark said. "The simplest definition is that we work to prepare the human species for the changes ahead."

"Changes? What kind of changes?"

Dark paused, a thoughtful expression. Joe glanced at the monitor. It looked pretty good. Dark had some skills, he thought.

"The changes that face us all may be various," Dark said. "Environmental changes, social changes. An asteroid or comet could strike the planet. We could be in the path of a deadly coronal mass ejection from the sun. War. Terrorism. We could move into outer space. There might be new social paradigms or new technologies that change us even more than capitalism, universal suffrage, indoor lighting, electricity, or computers."

"So the GPHH is involved in technology? Developing defense systems, alternative energy, that kind of thing?" Joe looked skeptical.

"We might do a little of that," Dark said. "But mostly we're interested in minds. We aim to expand the scope and ability of consciousness, so that we can understand and respond to the changes in our lives."

"And how exactly do you hope to accomplish this?"

"We're still working on that," Dark smiled. "Presently we have some written materials and a set of exercises that we practice."

"Exercises that make you physically fit?"

"Exercises that give you an understanding of your consciousness and some measure of control over your life. Exercises that teach your mind and body to perceive the world as magical."

"Okay." Joe copped a serious pose for the camera. "We've heard some allegations concerning your c-, uh, group." He paused, holding the pose for just a moment. "Do you practice sex magick?"

"Do I, personally, practice sex magick?" Dark asked.

"You personally, or your organization. Either answer will do for starters."

"What exactly do you mean by sex magick? There are a variety of practices that might be considered…"

"Occult practices," Joe said, "in which sex is involved."

"Yes."

"Yes? Miss Westheimer, um, Esty…" He paused. He momentarily felt inhibited. "Have you been indoctrinated into sex magick?"

"Of course." She smiled a little. "And I've gotten quite good."

Hoots, cheers, wolf whistles.

As the audience settled down, Esty leaned toward Joe and asked. "Can I say something to my mom?"

"Certainly," said Joe. "What message do you have for your mother?"

Esty turned to look at the camera. "Mom, I know you're watching," she said. "And I want you to know I'm all right and I'm here of my own free will. I'm finally getting an opportunity to contribute to something bigger than myself. We're going to change the world. Just wait, mom, you'll see and you'll be proud." She turned back to Joe and shrugged. "That's it, I guess. Thank you."

15 ✱ The Planetary Wank

Joe aimed his attention back at Damon Dark. "Tell us about your Founder."

The Astral Score played a fanfare.

Dark smiled. "A great man, a visionary and a leader. What do you want to know?"

"How did the Founder, um, found the Great Purple Hoo-Ha, Incorporated?"

"Oh, that's a fascinating story," Dark offered. "Our accounts of the Founding of the GPHH now fill eight volumes. Are you sure we have time?"

"How about the quick TV version?" Joe glanced at a monitor and read the time code. "Keep it under five minutes, forty seven seconds." He smiled politely.

"Back in the 20th Century," Dark jumped right in, "it was popular to encourage mass action of various non-effective kinds. For instance, there were rallies against war in which everyone took drugs and had sex. There were attempts to get all the nations of the world to say OM all at the same moment, on the theory that it would raise the vibration of the entire species. There were moments of world prayer for peace. Some of these were by design and some, it was said, were inflicted upon the planet whether humans chose them or not. For instance, the comets scheduled to visit and shower us with everything from poison gas to bliss and enlightenment. The various hyperwaves, vibratory realms, and space rays through which the Earth was set to blunder on its course through the universe. And of course, there were your major, long-standing, mainstream hoo-has, the Apocalypse, Ragnarok, Nuclear Winter, the Return of the Rock Stars, the Liftoff of the Lasagna. And so on. A hoo-ha of some sort or another every month or two. Hoo-has now, hoo-has to come."

The electric guitar fanfare was joined by a rhythm section and began building into a melody.

"The Founder, as a young man, was a true believer in all kinds of silly crap. He believed that any one of these mass hallucinations could save the universe, if only he and at least ninety-nine of his monkey-descended brethren would believe. He bravely awaited the coming of the space brothers, was planning to surf Time Wave Zero, and danced with thousands on a beach in Thailand as the Earth was enveloped by the Aztec Space Ray and everyone didn't get nearly as enlightened as planned."

Dark addressed the audience. "Does anyone remember the Planetary Wank?" There was only silence from the audience.

"That's because only a few people knew about it while it was actually happening. It wasn't a very well-known mass movement at all. The Founder saw a flyer about it, on a bulletin board in a laundromat. It made perfect sense, of course: If everyone on the planet took a moment, all at the same time, to masturbate – well, very simply, our hands would be busy and we wouldn't be able to pull triggers, push buttons that drop bombs, operate the controls of nasty pollution-spewing corporate machinery, or count money, not to mention many other heinous activities of modern life that involve hands. Everyone would have a moment of bliss all at the same time and then we'd all go wash up.

"The Founder took it very seriously, although some have remarked that in those days he was often looking for an opportunity to wank. Anyway, he took the flyer to Stinkos and made as many copies as he could afford – twelve – and he went to every other laundromat in town and hung them on bulletin boards or left them next to the stacks of old magazines in the customer seating area. He was confident that an army of wankers was spreading the news. If every one of his twelve flyers spawned another twelve, and each of those another twelve, it would be only days, maybe hours even, before everyone on Earth was preparing for the Planetary Wank."

A fanfare, pure and simple, then the rhythm section began to rock.

"Finally, the appointed time came – and so did the Founder, holding the thought in his mind of the bond that he was forming with millions of other humans, a bond of peace and love and shared experience, in a safe-sex kind of way. And at the climax of the hoo-ha, his directed imagination carried him to a goal of sorts. He was granted a momentary vision and direct connection to every single other person on the planet participating in the Planetary Wank. There were three, besides him: two teenage boys who had picked up flyers in laundromats while their mothers washed clothes, and the 73 year old woman, a part-time laundromat attendant, who had originally conceived of the plan.

"Along with the vision came a sudden understanding, a deep, internal certainty that there was a way to bring forth a hoo-ha of great, world-shaking power. A real hoo-ha, not a newage creation of fluff and love or a government propaganda creation of fear and duct tape, but a true evolutionary leap of human consciousness. A Great Purple Hoo-Ha. A leap that would carry our species into the unknown, into a future as incomprehensible to us as our world would be to a Neanderthal. And the Founder knew how to do it. He had a plan."

"That's a disgusting story," Joe said. "And if the GPHH had any real way to pull off a hoo-ha of such magnitude, it would disrupt our entire way of life, if I understand you correctly. A truly evolutionary shift of consciousness — whatever we are to take that to mean — would damn everyone who failed to adapt. That might be millions or even billions who would be unable to keep pace."

"Well, that's why we have to be prepared for the changes," Dark said mildly.

"Maybe some of us don't want changes in the first place," Joe said. "Maybe some of us like our lives just the way they are."

"There are always changes," Dark suggested. "We're choosing which ones we want to experience."

"What will it be, Mr. Dark? Total economic disaster? Complete collapse of the roads, the electrical grid, the infrastructure? Political revolution? Famine? Plague? Could it mean war?"

"No one knows, Joe," Dark said. "No one knows."

"I think someone knows more than they are telling," Joe continued. "The Founder must have some general objective. Are his aims for the benefit of mankind or does he mean to bring destruction of Biblical proportions?"

"You think Wilderman knows what form the Great Purple Hoo-Ha will take?"

Joe broke character for a moment. "What? Wilderman?"

There was that same guitar fanfare, jagged with distortion.

"Yes," said Dark. "The Founder, Wilderman. We've been talking about him for the last seven and a half minutes."

"Holy shitballs," Joe said.

Hoots, cheers, and applause.

✱ The Great Purple Hoo-Ha

16 ✶ Neurochemical Cascade

As the show ended to thunderous applause, Joe escorted his guests off the set. He was slightly distracted as his mind processed the information and the Astral Score oozed and swelled with atmospheric synthesizer, modern cousin to the Theremin. Wilderman was the Founder of Great Purple Hoo-Ha, Incorporated? That changed things a bit. Wilderman actually lived up to the legend, at least in one area that Joe knew. He could make a person, well, not exactly cream in their shorts, but have a damn nice jolt to the gonadic pleasure center, just by thinking or breathing or whatever. And he could teach the technique, as Marlena amply demonstrated. What other real mind tech did Wilderman have at his command? It made the whole idea of the hoo-ha just a little more plausible.

And Esty Westheimer really didn't seem like a brainwashed cultist. She seemed pretty and smart and she… He looked over at her. She was sipping water from a paper cup and looking in his direction. She lowered the cup and smiled. A deep bass note joined the astral ambience, sliding toward a rhythm.

He returned the smile, took a deep breath and started to walk over. Two paces and he was intercepted. The Astral Score ceased.

"Damn fine show," Jerry Hull bellowed heartily. "Some damn fine TV. The Sex Lives of Spies. I love it. Nice hooters! And you! You're at the top of your form, Joe. Incredible. You just keep 'em coming like this one. I knew you could do it. I never lost faith in you for a moment."

"Thanks, Jerry. I try."

"I don't know what you did, but it's working. You are The Man!" Jerry clapped Joe on the back.

"Fuck you, Jerry," Joe said. "Fuck you up the ass."

"It's my pleasure," Jerry said. "Right back at you!"

"Jerry, what did you think I just said?"

"Huh? You said 'Thank you, Jerry. Keep up the good work!'"

"No," said Joe. "I said 'Fuck you up the ass with a live eel.'"

"Right," said Jerry. 'Isn't that the same thing?"

"Sure, Jerry. Listen, gotta run. I'll see you on Monday, okay?"

"Right, right, Monday," Jerry was saying as Joe pushed on past. "Great stuff. Great stuff."

Esty was no longer in sight. Joe looked around and spotted her near the door, on her way out. A note on the astral bass, very low and very soft.

Almost every human on Planet Earth has another person living inside. That other person is our own Inner Babe. The Inner Babe is the projected complement of our identity and s/he is just as real as God, Santa Claus, or The President of the United States. When we meet someone who demonstrates enough of the qualities of our Inner Babe, a cascade of neurochemical change begins, eventually leading to that confusing and blissful state of consciousness called "love." The Inner Babe is not exactly an ideal form in the sense that Joe might have had a thing for slim young women with dark hair. Or that he deeply appreciated a firm round ass packed into tight jeans. While these may have been factors in the arousal of Joe's undeniable lust, it must be noted that recognition of the Inner Babe is more often based on subtle behavioral cues: a tone of voice, a tilt of the head, a repeated pattern of eye movements, a way of breathing, a whiff of pheromone, or a certain rhythm of movement. The cues just start to add up and – wham! The immediate effects of the neurochemical cocktail include rapid heartbeat, changes in breathing, distortions in perception of time, feelings of euphoria, and full-on sexual arousal.

Joe's short exposure to Esty Westheimer triggered off a mighty, rainbow-suffused waterfall of neurochemicals, not to mention a growing hard-on.

"Excuse me, Esty," he said as he caught up.

She turned and looked at him. The bass note slid into a rhythm: deep dub, surprisingly upbeat, yet full of soul and mystery. Joe noticed how clean her face was, how the smooth skin of her brow slid gracefully down to her nose, how the curve of her cheek made a perfect form with the lines of her chin.

Once enough Inner Babe cues have been recognized and the neurochemicals are doing their thing, the eager unconscious mind suddenly accepts this other person *as* your Inner Babe, projecting that feeling of completion upon every aspect of her or him. If your love raises his or her arm, it becomes the perfect Inner Babe arm raise. If the object of your affection sneezes, it is instantly transformed into a wonderful Inner Babe sneeze. If your outer babe sneaks out a stinky fart, it is, of course, an utterly delightful Inner Babe stinker.

To Joe, Esty's nostrils were absolutely the most perfect little holes ever to appear on anyone's head.

"Hi," she said. "I was going to, you know, stick around, but you looked like you were busy."

The most interesting situations, love-wise, are of course when both parties concerned (and, in some cases, when *all* parties concerned) have mistaken each other for their Inner Babes. Consciously there may be a sense of uncertainty or even disbelief, yet the unconscious mind, who has been having most of the fun all along, absolutely knows when Inner Babitude is returned. A feedback loop forms. The feelings intensify and unconscious recognition of the increased intensity in the other increases the intensity of your own feelings. Your Astral Score swells and may spontaneously take a flashy, prog-rock drum solo, with a rotating platform and pyrotechnics. At some point, although no outward, ordinary communication has been made, the feelings in both rise above a threshold and certainty is achieved on a conscious level.

"You want to get out of here?" Joe asked.

Esty nodded. "Yeah." Drums joined the Astral Score, a djembe holding steady with the dub.

The feedback loop of mutual Inner Babitute is quite powerful enough. When you add to it whatever it was that guy 'Adam' did to Joe's public image, the funhouse of mental mirrors in the carnival of love is open for business.

"You have an incredible ass," Joe said.

"Thank you," Esty replied. "I have great respect for you as well."

17 ✷ Schoolyard Magick

Humans have a variety of rituals they engage in to promote social bonding. Many of these rituals involve matching and mirroring each others' behavior. For instance, a handshake involves two people adopting similar postures and making simultaneous and nearly identical movements. The hands have fairly sensitive nerve endings and when two hands grasp each other, these same nerve endings are stimulated in each and each person experiences pretty much the same thing. Eating or drinking together promotes similar mirroring and social bonding and this can be clearly observed when two people sit opposite each other at a small table, lifting cups of stimulating beverages to the very sensitive nerve endings of their lips and tongues, often simultaneously.

Joe and Esty drank coffee together at a table for two in the back corner of an East Village eatery. As if on cue, they both looked up from their coffee and smiled at each other. A synth lick adorned the deep bass and drums.

"You're not quite what I expected," Joe said.

Esty laughed. "You're not what *I* expected. I didn't think I'd like you."

"Yeah, same here." They sipped for a moment. The astral dub rolled on. Far in the background, a low pitched Theremin offered sci-fi harmony.

When two humans mistake each other for their Inner Babes and begin to bond through social rituals, the feedback loop can accelerate quickly. Many panic at this stage and some bail out. The intensity of sensation suddenly opens the mind to neurological change. Neurons find new directions for their signals. Perceptions become imprinted on the brain. A touch can linger forever, long after the physical contact is gone, a chance word can become a reason to exist.

"I mean, I'm really glad we met," Esty said.

"Everyone tells me that, these days. And I'm also glad we met."

"What did you think I'd be like? Helpless cult victim?" They both laughed, just a little.

"We were all hoping," Joe said. "It makes for good TV."

"Sorry to let you down."

"So, how did you get involved in this, anyway? Your mom's version didn't go over too well with my producer, you know. Too Afternoon Special, not quite Jerry Springer enough."

"How did I get involved in the Great Purple Hoo-Ha?" Esty mused as the bass dropped out of the astral mix, leaving, once again, ambient waves of sound rising and falling on an auditory beach. "It was a boy."

"I should have known," Joe said.

"Marco Chang. How's that for a name? Italian mother, Chinese father. He was kind of cute, even with all the zits and the dental gear. During my free period I used to sit in the library. I'd pull books from the shelves and look through them. Sometimes something would catch my attention and I'd take the book home and read the whole thing, but I'd just kind of browse in there. I had a stack of books on the occult – witchcraft, shamanism, high magic. Stuff I'd read about, but was never quite moved enough to play around with. And then Marco came over and sat down.

"That's the first time he ever talked to me in school, I think. He had a couple of friends, I know, but you'd see him by himself just as often. And he'd seem comfortable by himself, reading a book or whatever. Anyway, he smiled like we were old friends and planted his ass in the chair across from me, just a little further away than you are now. He started shuffling through the stack of books saying, 'Oh, this is a good one' or 'This one's a bunch of bullshit.'

"Finally he said, 'Some of these are pretty good, but I've got one that's way better. The library doesn't have a copy.'

"From his bag he pulled out a tattered trade paperback. It was really filthy and beat up, though from what he said, it was a new book. 'I've been using it a lot,' he said. He showed me the cover, but wouldn't hand it over to me. It was called *'The Text of the Opener.'*

"When I asked him what it was, he said it was a method to develop real magick powers, a collection of exercises that gives the ability to perceive demons and angels, gods and goddesses, and entities not even mentioned in the old books. And to manifest things, make things happen.

"'And you've done this?' I asked. He smiled and flipped through the pages, showing me just how very used the book was.

"'And now you have magick powers?' I asked.

"'You could say that,' Marco answered.

"'Show me,' I said. 'Show me some real magick.'

"Marco thought for a moment. 'Okay,' he said. 'But not here. Tonight, meet me in the schoolyard.'

"I told my mom that I had a date with a boy, which was embarrassing, but easier to explain than what I hoped was really going to happen. And maybe I was hoping, a little, that it was really a date, too.

"The sun was setting behind the trees as I entered the schoolyard. The trees were blowing in the wind and the orangey sunlight was flickering through the branches. Marco was already there, sitting on some stone steps at the back of the building. The hood of his sweatshirt was pulled up and he was reading his book with a keychain flashlight. The glow reflected between his hooded face and the pages of the book made him look like a hobbit or an elf on some mystical business.

"'That you even came,' Marco said, 'shows that you are different from the rest. You are ready.'

"My first thought was, 'He's asked others and I'm the only one dumb enough to show.'

"'Are you ready to have the very foundations of your reality pulled out from beneath you?'

"'Sure,' I said. 'Why not?'

"'Okay.' He took a deep breath. 'This will take about five minutes. Just keep quiet 'til I'm done.'

"'You're going to do some magick, right now?'

"'Yeah. I'm just going to do something in my head. Then you'll tell me how you feel.'

"He arranged himself into a yoga posture on the top step. What little I could see of his face under the hood looked furrowed in concentration. He remained that way for a minute or so, then opened his eyes and took a peek at the book, closed them again and was off in his mind for a few more minutes. Then he opened his eyes and grinned at me.

"'Okay,' he asked, 'how do you feel?'

"'A little sleepy,' I said truthfully.

"'Is that all?' he asked.

"'Um, a little warm, maybe?'

"'Ah, that's the magick starting to work. I think.'

"'What's it supposed to do?'

"'I visualized you having an overwhelming urge to kiss me.'

"'You were trying to make me want to kiss you?'

"He grinned. 'Yeah. Did it work?'

"I hadn't had too many opportunities to kiss boys at that point in my life, so I decided to play along. I stepped closer to him. He stepped closer, lifted his face. I pulled back his hood and...

"...had an overwhelming urge to gag. Marco's mouth was wired with braces and retainers, none of it very clean. His tongue looked like a stray piece of bologna caught in the mouth of the trash disposal." She shivered in disgust and then laughed.

"He begged and pleaded, assured me that his orthodontist approved. Finally he just said, 'Well, the magick worked anyway.'

"'You've got to be kidding,' I said.

"'Sure it did. You wanted to kiss me. Before you saw...' He shrugged pathetically and gestured at his bulging mouth.

"I decided to change the subject, quickly. I grabbed *The Text of the Opener* and Marco's LED light and flipped open the book. 'Let me try one,' I said.

"The page I opened to was titled 'How to Summon the Opener.' Marco read it over my shoulder. 'Uh, Esty, I don't think that's a good one to start with. It's, uh, kind of complicated.'

"'So if I get it wrong,' I asked, 'something horrible will happen? I'll summon demons and monsters instead?'

"'Well, no,' said Marco. 'It probably just won't work. Even I still can't do that one and I can do everything else in the book.'

"I looked over the instructions, about a page of them. 'Looks pretty straightforward,' I said. 'I can follow this. Let me try.'

"'All right, but don't say I didn't warn you. Afterwards I'll show you some better stuff.'

"I was already reading. It made a lot of sense to me and felt quite natural, as if it were a natural bodily function, something my nervous system was designed to do, but for whatever reason never experienced before. I won't go into too much detail. It was a technique to gather together six qualities – attention, language, passion, fitting, trance, and making – and merge them together in an external form. The qualities began as memories, then the feelings were isolated and turned into colored shapes and the shapes merged together. It was like solving a puzzle in my mind. Suddenly it clicked into place and felt whole… and…"

Joe waited patiently as Esty found her words. Ambient astral sound rose and fell and washed around them.

"And there was a flash of light, like a strobe, and a woman was there, naked except for a kind of filmy sash. She was beautiful, with long black hair. And she was pregnant. *Really* pregnant. I mean, she looked like she was giving us a few moments of time between contractions.

"Marco saw her too, so it wasn't just my personal hallucination. He was freaked. His mouth was open, with all that entails, and his eyes were bugged out. I think he just never saw naked breasts before.

"The woman looked at me and smiled. 'Oh, it's you,' she said. 'Good. Might as well prepare.'

"'Prepare for what?' I asked.

"'For whatever,' the woman said.

"'How do I prepare for whatever?' I persisted.

"'For starters,' the woman said, 'the book that you hold, *The Text of the Opener*, I grant it to you. It is now your copy.'

"Marco protested, saying he had paid good money for it, but the woman roared and advanced on Marco, her belly heaving. The last we saw of Marco was his ass, disappearing around the corner of the building just as fast as he could run."

"Marco was afraid of pregnant women?" Joe asked.

"Probably, but she wasn't just any pregnant woman," Esty explained. "She was an apparition, a goddess of some kind, very powerful. You could see it in her eyes, in her wild hair. She sort of glowed. And whatever she was about to give birth to, I don't know, you could sort of sense its presence, as if the unborn baby were part of the conversation. She was The Opener."

"The Opener," said Joe. "Holy shit." Astral ambience rose to a crest, crashed and scattered.

"When Marco was gone, the woman turned back to me and gave me a kiss full on the mouth. She said, 'You'll do just fine.' There was another flash of light and then I was alone in the schoolyard, holding a book."

"At least you got to kiss *someone*," Joe said. "So what did you do then?"

"I went home and spent the next couple of years learning the material from the book."

"And what of Marco? Did you see him again?"

"I saw him in school, sure, but we didn't talk. Last I heard he was a born-again powerlifter on a crusade against the occult."

"Oh, really?" Joe asked. "Got any idea how to get in touch with him?"

18 ✶ Up and Down

Coffee finished, Joe and Esty wandered out onto the street. The Village was a carnival of straights, freaks of every stripe, out-of-towners, street vendors with choice yard sale items arranged on blankets, and business-as-usual, roaring, honking, cursing New York City traffic. Even though darkness had descended long ago, the more persistent street vendors were still standing by their wares, perhaps also offering late night contraband. The dub rhythm had returned, more subdued than before, yet holding promise of rocking with revelations to come.

"So will you show me something?" Joe asked.

Esty stopped, turned toward him and grabbed the front of her sweater. "What? Here?" She grinned.

"Save it for the show," Joe said. "I meant, I don't know, magick, an exercise from the book. Whatever you can show me."

She led him up a short set of stone steps into a marble courtyard next to an office building. "Okay," she said, "this is really basic. Can you lift me up?" She raised her arms. Joe hesitated for a moment, grinned and then placed his hands on Esty's waist. She felt firm and warm in his grip. He lifted her about a foot and a half off the ground and gently set her back down.

"Now lift me again," she said, closing her eyes. Joe lifted again, but he was either suddenly very weak or Esty was suddenly very, very heavy. He lifted her barely an inch and then had to set her back down from exhaustion. Far away but drawing closer, the astral Theremin.

"You wore me out the first time," he complained.

"I don't think so," Esty said. "Lift me again."

He held her and lifted her and she shot up, as light as a feather, over three feet off the ground. He felt like he could hold her there indefinitely.

"Okay, that was weird," Joe said. "It has something to do with the order that we're doing them in."

"I don't think so," Esty said, and they repeated the experiment in every possible combination of order, with the same results. When Esty wanted to be lifted, she rose up with very little effort from Joe and when she didn't want to be lifted, she was glued to the heavy stone of the courtyard. The Theremin was gathering a melody around the dub rhythm.

"It has something to do with the way you're asking me to hold you," Joe suggested.

Esty shook her head. "I don't think so," she said, and they repeated the experiment with Joe holding her in a variety of ways. The results were the same and they additionally learned that they very much liked to hold each other. They were also drawing a small crowd of those who had been using the courtyard as a rest stop or a living room. The astral Theremin wound up its solo and sank back into the dub.

"Do you want to know what I'm doing?" Esty finally asked.

"Levitating and, uh, unlevitating?"

Esty chuckled. "Something like that. When I want to go up, I place my attention way up in the sky, up in the clouds, or maybe even in the stars. When I want to stay down, I place my attention way down in the center of the Earth. It's as simple as that. Want to try?"

They picked out two large and relatively sober men from among the watchers and Esty stood them on either side of Joe. She instructed Joe to hold his arms bent at his sides and the two men grabbed him by the elbows, lifted him about two feet off the ground, then set him back down. At Esty's instruction, Joe placed his attention way down in the center of the Earth, imagining dense metals under extreme pressure, the massive gravitational anchor of a planet. And the two men strained to lift him barely two inches off the ground. Joe placed his attention up in the wispy clouds floating high, high above New York and suddenly he was airborne to a brief reprise of the Theremin melody. The men lifted him until their arms were fully extended above their heads, then, laughing with disbelief, set him gently back down.

Joe shook some hands and signed an autograph and they eventually managed to disengage and head up the street.

"Assuming you weren't in cahoots with those two, that's impressive," Joe said.

"Cahoots? What's that supposed to mean? We picked them out of the crowd."

"The Great Purple Hoo-Ha could have its agents everywhere. They could have followed us, just to prove a point."

"Um, I don't think so."

"Yeah, yeah," said Joe, "Okay, it's impressive, but what does it mean? What can you do with it?"

"They say it has all sorts of uses in the martial arts," Esty said, "but mostly it's about changing the way you think about the world. The way you place your attention in the world around you changes the way you interact with your world. How does it happen? What makes it happen? I don't know. You have to accept some ambiguity when you're at the fringes of your own experience. Observe and suspend judgment. It starts to make a lot of sense when you take it along with the other exercises." She stopped suddenly and Astral Score paused with her. "Shit!"

"What's wrong?"

"What time is it?"

"Eleven twenty."

"The last train to Poughkeepsie is eleven thirty. Think I can make it to Grand Central in time, from here?"

"Not a chance," Joe said.

"How will I get home?"

"Stay overnight at my place and I'll have the studio send a limo for you in the morning. It'll work out nicely because I have this amazing, overwhelming urge to kiss you."

"That's not my doing," Esty said.

"Oh yes it is." The dub bass kicked back in, full and deep.

The first kiss was a quick one, a moment of lip contact. Exactly at that moment, a taxi pulled up and the driver called, "You need a cab?" They hopped in and were gone.

19 ✱ Reverse Peristalsis

"This is great," Esty said, as they settled into their seats. "The cab showed up exactly when we needed it."

"Oh, I could have waited another minute or so," Joe commented.

"It's a good omen," Esty went on. "When you're on the right track, magically speaking, the universe seems like it lends a hand."

"I was thinking more about lips," Joe said, taking her hand, "but hands are nice, too."

She smiled. "Now that you mention it, hands and lips – both pretty nice."

Their hands pulled them toward each other, lips drawing closer, Astral Score swelling.

"Hey," the cabbie said loudly and cheerfully, all but extinguishing the Score, "you're that guy from TV, am I right? Joe… Schmoe! Right! That's who you are!"

"Fuck you and I hope your hemorrhoids bleed into the upholstery," Joe said.

Esty gaped at him. The cab driver smiled and said. "See! I knew it. I know TV, yessir. You ask me any question about TV, I'll tell ya."

"How many TVs can you cram up your ass?" Joe asked. "You fucking moron."

"Oh, I know the answer to that," the cabbie said. "What's his name, Mark Layton. Right?"

Esty shook her head in disbelief.

"You are one ugly sonofabitch, you know that?" Joe continued.

"Well thank you," the cabbie replied. "I spend a lot of time working at it, you know, watching."

"Oooh, I want to try one," Esty said.

"Esty, no…"

"Hey cabbie, you have the most enormous ass I've ever seen on a human being," Esty said.

"Fuck you, lady," the cabbie said. "That's hurtful."

"It only works for me, Esty," Joe whispered. "I'll explain later." To the cabbie he said, "It's hurtful that any of us have to look at your fat ass."

"Oh, well, then," the cabbie said more sweetly. "I'm sorry miss. I didn't understand."

Esty laughed. "That's incredible," she said. Impulsively they grabbed for each other, lips were drawn magnetically together, half a note of dub bass, and suddenly the cab driver slammed on the brakes and they were knocked from their seats. A black sedan with a flashing red light on the roof raced across their path, siren screaming, collision narrowly avoided by the cabbie's fast footwork.

"He's going our way," the cabbie enthused, swerving out to follow the limo. "He'll clear out some road. You just hang on back there, folks. We're all gettin' lucky tonight."

The cab's insufficient suspension slammed and banged over potholes and manhole covers as they surfed the wake of the black car. They hauled ass a few blocks uptown and suddenly lost track of the sedan. But it didn't matter; they were at Joe's door. Joe paid, autographed the cab's cardboard pine tree air freshener, and they went inside.

Joe's place was spacious and well-lit. It had great views of the city on two sides. The furniture was expensive and fairly new. And it was all covered with the glorious and reeking residue of Joe's existence. Dead cold pizza oozed grease through the seams of its box, dripping in shiny orange streaks down the front of a maple wood cabinet. Clumps of fetid laundry dotted the hardwood floor at irregular intervals. Peanut shells, popcorn husks and crushed tortilla chips oozed from under the cushions of a fabulous leather sofa. Empty wrappers, dirty dishes, mangled newspapers and magazines, and a thick layer of unidentifiable grime were spread unevenly on most surfaces. And that was just the living room.

Esty looked at the mess and began to reflexively recoil in horror, but she looked at Joe and, of course, looking at Joe changed everything and the funk was momentarily forgotten. Joe looked at Esty and, closing the door behind him, finally scooped her into his arms for a long awaited kiss. Astral dub resumed as their bodies pressed warmly together, their lips met – and Joe's phone began to ring.

"Goddamn," he muttered, retrieving the phone and checking the caller ID, "It's my producer. I've got to take this." He answered the phone. "Hey, Jerry, what's up?"

Jerry's voice was more subdued than usual. The dub disappeared, leaving only a hint of dubious Theremin. "Joe, uh, we got a phone call at the office a few minutes ago…"

"Yes, Jerry, what is it?"

"It was hard to understand and… and…"

"And what?"

"The voice. It was… my secretary answered the phone… I… I think she might need help…"

"Your secretary? It's almost midnight."

"The voice said... someone... or something... was coming to find you. Tonight. It was... horrible..."

"Jerry, be a man, okay? What was so fucking horrible?"

"I can't describe it. The voice was... disgusting..." Jerry moaned in real agony at the recollection of the voice. "Rebecca's still crying. I'm..."

"It must have said who it was, Jerry."

"Maybe when she calms down, she'll remember... I... I couldn't understand... I just wanted to blow chunks, Joe, but I couldn't stop listening. Rebecca only stopped because I yanked the phone away from her."

"Are you on acid?"

"No, Joe, well only a little left over from yesterday."

"Please, Jerry, I've got someone over here. Please don't call me unless it's a real emergency. Okay?"

"That voice... will haunt my dreams..." Joe switched off the phone.

He sighed and gave Esty a quick, exasperated recap of Jerry's call. She had cleared a space on the sofa and sat with her legs tucked under her. He pushed a collection of slightly sticky junk food wrappers to one side, to make room for his own butt.

"Would you like something to drink?" Joe asked. "I've got wine and Old Mystery."

"No thanks, I rarely drink," Esty said. "And besides, I'm underage."

"I keep forgetting that," Joe said. "You seem just the right age to me."

"How about something to smoke?" Esty asked, producing an irregularly-shaped cone of paper. The dub was sneaking back as reggae.

"So it was true about the drugs," Joe said.

Esty laughed. "What drugs? It's a doobie. You want some?"

They sat close together on the sofa and shared a bit of the spliff. Esty carefully tamped the remainder and set it to rest on top of an empty Merkin can. A moment later they were sliding gratefully, at last, into each others' arms.

There was a pounding at the door.

Joe jumped to his feet and ran to look out the peephole. Esty hid the roach under the remains of an old Schnitz cracker box.

Through the fisheye lens of the peephole, Joe could make out the distorted nose, eyes and forehead of a nervous-looking white man and shadows that suggested someone beyond him. Joe cracked the door to the limits of the chain bolt. "Can I help you?"

"Holy crap," the man said. "It really is you. I was hoping. This job can be really interesting."

"What do you want?"

"Homeland Security," the man said. "I'm Agent Fergus and this is Agent Twackham. May we come in?" A military snare drum rattled and snapped astrally.

"Say please, assholes."

"Oh, certainly, yes, may we please come in and I might add we do have the authority to break your door down if necessary."

"Fuck you," Joe replied, unfastening the door and admitting the men.

Agent Fergus was small and nervous, and his nose actually was large, it wasn't just a trick of the peephole, Joe noted. Agent Twackham was also small and nervous and his nose was actually even larger.

"What is this about?" Joe asked.

"We are investigating the presence of an unscheduled jet aircraft now approaching New York airspace," Fergus stated gravely. Do you know anything about a jet airplane?"

"Not a thing," Joe said, "so you can be on your way now." He tried to hustle them back to the door, but they evaded him and wandered into the living room. Agent Fergus nodded grimly to Esty.

"Then how come it said your name?" Agent Twackham picked up the investigation.

"How come what said my name?"

"The jet airplane," said Twackham.

"We received one transmission from the plane," Fergus elaborated. "It said a whole lot of things that no one could really understand – or listen to – but the one thing we all agreed on was that it said, 'I'm coming for Joe.'"

"So what?" said Joe. "There must be a million Joes in New York."

"Oh come now," said Twackham. "You're *the* Joe. If you think 'New York' and 'Joe,' well, that's you."

"Especially after that show tonight," Fergus gushed. "Amazing. And I know plenty of spies. It's all true."

"You liked the show tonight?" Joe asked.

They all heartily agreed it was a great show, including Esty.

"I mean, really," Joe said, "you're not just saying that because…" He shook his head.

"Because why?" Esty asked.

"Never mind."

"So you know nothing about this airplane? It's approaching the city even as we speak. Fighter jets are scrambled and ready to intercept," Twackham said.

"Maybe it has something to do with the phone call," Joe said, and explained about the call he received from Jerry.

The two agents made some gruff noises at each other, jotted some notes on tiny little pads, and turned to go.

"We're locking down this street," Fergus said. "Security teams will be deployed both outside and inside your building."

"For your protection," Twackham added.

"Yeah, that's right," Fergus said sincerely. "We're big fans."

The agents stomped out the door and Joe flipped all the locks shut. He stalked back to the sofa, a tentative astral bass note sliding gratefully back into full dub as he sat close to Esty and took her into his…

This time it was Esty's phone that spoiled the fun and whipped the phonograph needle across the grooves of the Astral Score. She sighed and flipped it open.

"Mom?!" she said in disbelief. "You haven't called me in over a year… You saw the show? Uh huh. Yes, I meant it. No, I'm still in New York. In the city, yes. What? The news? Terrorists? I know, mom. I think it's a mistake, a false alarm or something. Mom… Mom… I'll call you back tomorrow, okay? Mom… I promise… I'll call you back… Mom! I will call you back tomorrow!" Esty clicked the phone shut.

She turned her attention back to Joe. A tenuous query of a bass note.

"She saw the show," Esty said. "And she's been watching the news, too. Something about a terrorist jet approaching New York."

From outside, winnowing its way in through triple glazing and security doors, they could hear horns, sirens, and shouts.

"Fuck it," said Joe. "Who knows when we'll get another chance?" He took Esty in his arms. An astral flourish of drums and the dub was rolling on again.

"You're such a romantic," she said sincerely as their lips met and...

Joe's phone rang again and an astral wet blanket instantly muffled the Astral Score.

"Shit! What now?" He looked at his phone, which said only "Cellular Caller." Faintly, but growing rapidly along with Joe's heartbeat: ominous astral timpani drums.

"What is it?" Esty asked.

"It's just those drums," Joe said.

"You... can hear the Astral Score?" Esty asked, amazed.

The phone was still ringing and the good, old Theremin was weaving weird electronic magic into the drum rhythm.

Joe nodded and finally answered the phone. The Astral Score ceased and Joe heard a familiar, phlegmy voice. "Hello? Joe? Is that you?" It was Rex Massenclear.

Esty was staring with a look of horror.

"Rex!" Joe said. "To what do I owe the pleasure?"

"I saw the show. You were right, we need to talk. I'm on my way."

"On your way? What? How?"

"My plane just landed. I'll be there soon."

"New York is a madhouse tonight, Rex. Are you taking a cab?"

"I'll be there in, uh, twenty minutes," Rex said.

"Do you know how to get here? Do you…." The line was dead.

Esty was still staring and the Astral Score was silent.

"It was Rex Massenclear," Joe said. "Do you know him? 'Yo Momma Smoked My Blunt'? He's on his way here."

Esty stared. "That voice," she said. "That horrible…" She shuddered.

"You could hear Rex?" Joe asked. "Through my phone?" He shook his head. "Everyone thinks he's so disgusting. I can't figure it out. He's nasty, yeah, but not *that* bad."

"It was him," Esty said. "Your producer's phone call. The jet plane approaching New York."

"What? You think Rex is a terrorist?"

"No, but that voice," she shuddered again. "It's as awful as Jerry said and I didn't even get a real earful."

"What? You think so? He's a little phlegmy, I think, but…"

"A little phlegmy? Was he even using his mouth to talk? It sounded like someone blowing bubbles of phlegm out his ass! It sounded like the belly of a whale who's eaten sewage instead of plankton and wants to puke and shit at the same time! It was like the sound an enormous pimple would make as it bursts and floods half the city!"

"Really," Joe said, glancing at his tiny plastic phone. "It's not that bad."

She shuddered yet again and Joe shook his head.

"But hey," Esty said, gathering her wits. "You can hear the Astral Score."

"Yeah, ever since I met Adam."

"Adam? I learned to hear it from Wilderman."

"That figures. Have you been hearing the Theremin?"

"The weird science fictiony thing? Yeah. I like it. But what I really like is that dub theme."

"Dub?"

An astral bass note. "Dub," Esty said, sliding closer to Joe. He leaned toward her and the bass note stretched out, bounced back and eased into a deep cosmic groove.

"Oh yeah," Joe said. "I like that one." Their arms wrapped around each other, their lips actually pressed together…

And Joe's phone rang again and the astral rhythm train was derailed. "Goddammit." He grabbed the phone and thumbed it on. "Hello."

"Joe!" It was Jerry. "We've got it! We've got the name!"

"Jerry, what name?"

"The phone call. Rebecca remembered what she heard. She's still a bit traumatized from the experience of retrieving the memory. We had to…"

"Jerry! What's the fucking name?"

"Rex Massenclear."

"Tell me something I don't know. Jerry, absolutely just leave me alone tonight, okay?" Joe clicked off the phone. He sighed deeply.

He turned back to Esty who was glaring impatiently. "No more phones," she said.

"No more phones," said Joe.

They turned off their phones. Outside, the sounds of sirens, horns, and voices were increasing. Esty removed her sweater. She wore a tight black tank top, the final layer of clothing on her upper body. Joe took a deep breath and suddenly the full dub mix was on again, deep and mighty, raising the vibration of one and all. In a moment they were in each other's arms.

When the feedback loop of Inner Babitude is complemented by the kind of influence on other people that Joe exhibited, it can be quite intense and they were already reveling in the pull that it created between them. And then, as the bass rocked the astral plane, as they actually began to touch each other and give all their attention to each other, the intensity of feelings shared by Joe and Esty increased by an order of magnitude. This was something else entirely, a new component in the brew of neurochemicals and magick, and it began with Esty; tendrils of nearly-tangible energy, colored strands of singing, vibrating, shimmering stuff, reached and meshed between them. Outside, the sirens and horns seemed to reach a crescendo. Rumbling and banging could be heard from elsewhere in the building. They kissed, their hands exploring beneath their shirts. A cascade of green and gold light shimmered between them and the dub pulled their minds from primal urges to mystical heights and back again. Joe's hand felt the warm curve of Esty's breast. There were loud footsteps and shouting in the hallway outside the apartment.

They moved against each other with the deep urgency of the dub and the colors that bound them together grew richer, more vibrant. Esty's hand strayed down the front of Joe's pants. His fingers stroked her surprisingly erect nipple. The dub bass boomed enough to almost drown out the timpani drums, and almost enough to keep them from hearing the apartment door being smashed in.

They released each other and jumped to their feet, the colored tendrils instantly fading away and the bass halting in mid beat. As Agents Fergus and Twackham appeared in a cloud of splintered door and wallboard dust, all that remained of the Astral Score was the distant, gradually rising rumble of the timpani. From outside could be heard a different rumble: an approaching wave of truck engines, sirens, horns, and shouts.

"Where's the weed?!" Twackham demanded.

Joe and Esty gave innocent looks and shrugged.

"We smelled it when we were in here before. Where is it?"

"It's just a roach," Esty said, surrendering the remains of the doobie.

"Oh thank the gods," said Twackham, producing a Zippo lighter from a suit pocket and igniting the roach. He took a deep toke while Fergus waited impatiently for his turn.

"You broke the door down for a toke?" Joe asked. "That's fucking sad."

Twackham finally exhaled and said, "It's coming. Here."

"It?" Joe shook his head. "It's just Rex. Rex Massenclear. The musician?"

"No," Fergus stammered. "It's... It's... awful. Disgusting. It's... not human." He filled his lungs with ganja smoke.

"I thought you were going to shoot down his jet." Joe said.

"The pilots are instructed to try to make visual contact first. They... they did." Twackham said. "The fighter planes went down over Pennsylvania. They're searching for the pilots. We shut down JFK and the jet landed there. Private jet.

Custom paint job. Only one... person... aboard, as far as we could tell."

"It was Rex, right?"

"It... from what I heard...," Twackham continued, "the NYPD SWAT team was entirely incapacitated, instantly. There was mass panic in the airport, hundreds were taken sick."

"Taken sick?" Joe asked incredulously. "It's just Rex."

"John F. Kennedy International Airport will reek of vomit for years to come," Twackham said. "They'll never be able to clean it all out."

Timpani drums and the high tide of street noises were drawing closer. Amid the vehicles and sirens could be heard cries of anguish and a sound heard rarely on Planet Earth: the mass regurgitation by tens of thousands of New Yorkers of their dinners, snacks, drinks, and everything else regurgitatible.

"He's almost here," Fergus panicked . "He's almost here! Why are we still here? We've got to get out of here."

"Get a hold of yourself, man," Twackham said, puffing on what was left of the roach. "We have to secure the premises. If the troops in the corridor don't make it, we'll be the last line of defense between Joe and that... thing."

"You don't have to protect me from Rex," Joe said.

"Someone's got to protect you, Joe," Twackham said. "You're our city's treasure."

"Okay. I think I can do it," Fergus said, gritting his teeth. "I'll stay. I'll... stay!" He clenched the back of a chair as if it might anchor him to the spot when his feet decided to run.

Outside in the street: chaos. The drums were like approaching thunder. The screams and cries were beginning to drown out the engines and sirens. The wave of disgust broke against the building in a crescendo of coughing, crying, spewing, and moaning. The thundering roll of the timpani was nearing a peak and from within the building could be heard footsteps, banging, shouts, and every manner of reverse peristalsis.

The commotion rose up through the building to Joe's corridor, where waiting troops were reduced to retching, ineffective pools of jelly. Agents Twackham and Fergus drew weapons and braced themselves for action. The astral timpani drums built to an earth-shaking climax and then, abruptly, ceased.

And Rex Massenclear strode calmly through the ruined doorway.

Rex wore black jeans and a leather bomber jacket, open over a food-stained t-shirt. He was grimy, sweaty, and generally ungainly. His eyes were bloodshot and his hair a matted mess. He had apparently stepped in dogshit on the way over – one of his leather motorcycle boots was spattered with goopy brown and the scent wafted into the room with him.

The Homeland Security agents screamed, dropped their weapons, and ran – straight into a wall. They dropped to the floor, cowering, moaning, and heaving up the contents of their stomachs. A look of horror on her face, Esty climbed over the back of the couch and hid in the dirty laundry, her presence betrayed by choking and sobs.

"Hi, Rex," Joe said. "Come on in."

20 ✶ Monkeys

They shook hands and Rex settled into an armchair full of ancient Chinese food wrappers and old socks. "This place is disgusting," he commented mildly.

"What's with them?" Joe asked, gesturing at the quivering remains of Agents Twackham and Fergus. "What's with everybody?"

"Part of the deal I made," Rex said. "You made a slightly different deal, I gather."

"With Adam, you mean."

"I thought you were saying 'Adam' on the phone. That's why I blew you off. 'Atem.' You obviously have met Atem."

"Atem. Ay Tee Ee Em? Okay, this is beginning to make a little bit of sense, in a bent kind of way. The card..."

"You read the invocation on one of Wilderman's cards? And then you met Atem?"

"Something like that," Joe said, a dim light dawning in his mind. "Yeah."

"When I saw the show tonight, I knew you'd been tweaked. Atem has changed your neurology, my friend. That's obvious enough." Rex coughed a phlegmy cough. "Got anything to drink?"

Joe poured them each a shot of O.M.

"Thanks," said Rex. "I've got a bit of a cold and this stuff really cuts the snot." He poured the booze into his throat, sighed, coughed a couple times, blew his nose, and then looked back up at Joe. "What's your deal, Joe? I watched the show and saw how everyone reacted to you. When they see you or hear you they see and hear you as good, noble, wonderful? Is that it? I almost went for that one."

"It was Atem's decision," Joe said. "And he told me a little bit about you. I didn't really believe it. It's true, and even more than he said. I mean…" He gestured at the wreckage.

"Yeah." Rex burped mildly. "The effect has increased with time. When it all started, I seemed disgusting to people, but they could at least stay in the same room. I could still sell tickets, you know. Hell, I even had groupies who really got off on the whole grossness thing. I could still party. That's why I wanted to be a rock star. I wanted to party. I wanted the hot babes. And I had them, for about a year and a half. Then it really started to escalate. People would pass out, choke, gag, toss their cookies, lose their lunch. Now it's become dangerous. I can't even go out. I spread devastation wherever I go. You saw what happened."

"If my, um, gift from Atem also escalates," Joe mused, "they'll elect me god in under five years!"

"Careful what you wish for," Rex said. "You'll cause just as much wreckage."

"We seem to be immune to each other," Joe said. "You're kind of a gross guy, but, hey, I'm not tossing my fucking cookies over you."

"I have gotten a little gross," Rex explained. "I think seeing the reactions in others, understanding their expectations – it's rubbed off on me. I've started to *become* what they see me as. That and the isolation. This is the first real, face to face, conversation I've had in almost a year. Who cares if I pick my nose now? No one's going to see it.

"And likewise," Rex continued, shifting a bit in his seat to fart on a kung pao-smeared gym sock, "you don't seem very good and noble to me. Hell, I think you're really more disgusting than I am. What the hell is this thing I just farted on?"

"Fuck you," Joe observed. "So just what did Atem do to us?"

Rex blew his nose, poured himself an Old Mystery, blew his nose again, drank his shot, sighed, belched, and said, "I asked Wilderman about that. He told me about monkeys."

"Monkeys?"

"In the late 1980s there was a group of Italian scientists working with monkeys. They inserted electrodes into the brains of the monkeys to study their motor neurons, Wilderman said, the neurons activated, in particular, when a monkey reached for a piece of fruit. They had a bowl of fruit in front of the wired monkey and when the little guy would grab a banana, the motor neurons would go beep or something. Funny thing was, during a break in the experiment, one of the researchers reached for a banana. The monkey was watching and even though it was only watching, the same neurons did their thing."

"Monkey see, monkey do?"

"Yeah, yeah, everyone says that. Point is, when the monkey saw a big monkey take a banana, it was trying the action on for size in its imagination. It was thinking about what it would be like to do what the researcher was doing. Hell, it was probably thinking, 'That's my damn banana, you big weird monkey!' Anyway, we have much the same neurology as the monkeys and apes. When we watch someone else do something, we empathize with them a little – or a lot. Our brains fire off the same neurons as if we were doing what they are doing. They called them 'mirror neurons.' We use them to build a little mental model of the other person and then try it on for size. It's why we watch sports or movies. You see someone doing something amazing up on the big screen, you share in their feelings and triumphs. It explains a wide range of human phenomena, from contagious yawning to air guitar."

"So Atem did something to our mirror neurons?"

"It's not quite that simple." Rex blew his nose again. "Atem changed something in us that gives us specific influence over the mirror neurons of others. When they look at us or listen to us and build their little mental models of us, they build them in very specific ways. In my case, they are mixing me up with their own disgust for themselves, in your case they are confusing you with their own better natures. Wilderman said the change in me – in us – might be something tiny, the way some muscles are held, or a slight shift in posture, or any of a zillion other subtle cues that we project."

"I'm not sure I understand how a change in my posture could account for any of this. Or how Atem could have made the change. He just talked to me."

"Just talked, I like that." Rex sneezed into his hands and then wiped them on his jeans. "We 'just' talk to each other all the time in ways that make permanent changes. Haven't you ever heard something that inspired you? Or that fueled your hatred and defined your actions? Or what if that cutie choking behind the sofa told you she loved you? Would that change you?"

A choked moan issued from behind the sofa.

"It would change the things I do, certainly."

"And would people respond differently to you?"

"Perhaps," Joe said. "But that's more of a general response. They might catch a little of my frustration or elation. I can understand that. This..." He gestured back and forth at the two of them. "...is something more. How could anyone even figure out what to tweak?"

"You know the butterfly's wing theory?" Rex asked.

"That systems are so inter-related and complex that the beating of a butterfly's wing in one part of the world could lead to a hurricane somewhere else?"

"That's the one. Atem works like the butterfly. Only he's a smart-ass butterfly. He knows just where to beat his wing to cause a hurricane – or whatever – exactly where he wants it. A single word, said at just the right moment might be all it takes, with Atem's advanced knowledge. It's too complex for a single human mind." Rex coughed, filled a kleenex with gooey stuff, and poured himself another drink. A wild-eyed soldier appeared in the wrecked doorway, grew even more wild-eyed upon seeing Rex, and fell gasping out of sight.

"So how does Atem do it?"

"In case you haven't figured it out yet, he's not human. Or rather, humans are a part of him, many humans, and much else. He's a god of sorts, a modern god created by media and memetics."

"If he's not real..." Joe struggled with the problem.

"He's real enough," Rex said. "Oh yes, the Opener is very real."

"The Opener?"

"Yes, it's sort of Atem's job title."

"Atem is the Opener?"

"That's what I said."

There was louder choking and moaning from behind the sofa.

"I thought the Opener was a woman, a pregnant woman."

Rex leaned forward, scratched a zit on the underside of his cheek and cleared his throat, which turned into a major operation. Finally he said, "The Opener isn't a man or a woman. It's pure information rolling through our minds. It can appear any way it'd like. To whom did Atem appear as a woman?"

Joe nodded toward the sofa.

"Ah," said Rex. "Obviously she wasn't tweaked, though."

"She's not immune to us, at any rate," Joe clarified.

A sob and a choke from behind the sofa. Rex nodded and polished off his drink.

"Do you think Atem can, um, fix you?" Joe asked.

"I'm sure he can," Rex lamented, "but he won't. I've asked him."

"You asked him?"

"A hundred times. He says there's still a purpose in it. I can only imagine…"

"Something to do with the Great Purple Hoo-Ha?" Joe asked. "If your, um, tweak gets any more powerful, it might not take much more than that. You could, er, purge the entire world. Imagine if you were broadcast somehow, even now. It could mean devastation on a global scale."

Rex shook his head sadly. "Well, this has been a lovely chat. Satisfied my curiosity, at any rate. We're kindred souls, Joe. The most disgusting man in the world and the most wonderful. And we're really very much alike, though only we can know that. There's more to come, but I think I should spare your friends here, for now. They've been indisposed long enough." Rex stood and brushed well-aged crumbs of General Tso's chicken from the back of his legs.

"Wait," said Joe. "I still need to know something. How do I contact Atem again?"

"How'd you do it the first time?" Rex turned, coughed, farted, coughed again, sneezed, and then strode out the door.

The Great Purple Hoo-Ha

21 ✶ Not Yet

After a moment, gasping and sputtering, Agents Twackham and Fergus separated themselves from the debris on the floor and made lame attempts to wipe the barf from their dark suits. Esty crawled weakly from behind the sofa. In the corridor, groggy, puke-encrusted soldiers stood and checked their equipment. Outside, cries, shouting, horns and general mayhem resumed and the wave of mass peristalsis now flowed back toward JFK, the deep roll of astral timpani drums gradually receding into the distance.

"What…?" wheezed Twackham.

"Who…?" coughed Fergus.

"I told you," said Joe. "It's just Rex Massenclear, the most disgusting rock star ever."

"He is sooooo disgusting," said Twackham.

"Just let him get back to his plane and go home. I think he'll stay out of sight for now."

"Good plan," said Twackham. "He's not a threat."

"Unless you've just eaten," Esty added.

Twackham and Fergus got busy on their cell phones and wandered out into the corridor.

"How could you just sit there?" asked Esty. "And just calmly *talk* to him? I mean, holy shit! That was… that was…"

"Really disgusting?" Joe suggested.

"Yeah, disgusting."

"How much of our conversation did you hear?"

"All of it, I think," Esty said. "But…. Ewwwwwww!"

"So you understand how Rex and I affect other people?"

"Sure… like what you did in the cab, insulting the driver and he thought it was high praise. The Opener…"

"The Opener tweaked me. And he tweaked Rex. But she didn't tweak you."

"Thank the gods," Esty said. "Thank the gods."

Joe sat on the couch, blithely ignoring the soldiers peering in through the ruined doorway, and patted the cushion beside him. "So where were we?"

"Joe," Esty said queasily, "I feel a bit, erp, drained. I'd just like to go to sleep now, if that's okay."

"Ah well," Joe said. "I figured as much."

"It's not our time," Esty said. "Not yet."

22 ✶ QYFJ

After seeing Esty onto a morning train bound for Poughkeepsie, Joe returned to his building, shook and signed his way through a small mob, then went up to his apartment to find that a police contractor had created a temporary door from scraps of plywood. An eye-hook held it closed behind him and he had at least a modicum of privacy from the chaos and cleanup elsewhere in the building.

He rummaged through a pile of laundry, rifling the pockets of a mud and booze-spattered suit while ignoring the increasing reek of barf that filled the air. Soon he had what he sought, the now tattered and bent Invocation of Atem card. An astral Theremin could be heard, as if from afar. He planted his ass on the sofa, part of his mind noting that it was where Esty had sat last night. The thought shuffled up a deck of memories: the feel of her skin, the brief touch of her lips, the smell of her hair and body. Each memory flipped back into the pack, ready for the next deal and his attention returned to the tiny square of cardboard.

He read out loud, the astral Theremin rising in volume as he continued:

> *I offer my attention, the force of my consciousness, to Atem. I do this by speaking these words and allowing my understanding of them to develop. I charge these words with my emotions, with the power of my wants and needs, the feelings of my gains and losses, my joy, sorrow, love, anger, enthusiasm, melancholy, and elation. I start right where I am now, with the things I have close to hand,*

the thoughts and tools that already fit into my life. I ask that my experience of the world can change so that I can better make use of my thoughts and tools. I hope to notice you, Atem, in every way that you manifest in my life.

There was a flash of light, like a strobe, and a sound like a long strip of Velcro suddenly and quickly pulled apart. The Astral Score kicked in with a techno rhythm, the loopy sci-fi movie theme riding it up and down like an electronic roller coaster. And there he was, looking somehow very ordinary: a young man with tousled, dark hair, carrying a large gray cat.

Atem looked around. "You live here? What is that smell?" He sniffed. "Ah, Rex was here. Good."

On their first meeting, Joe had been full of Old Mystery and Atem had seemed very, very real, indistinguishable from another human being. This time, reasonably sober, Atem still seemed quite human and solid, yet if Joe looked closely, really made an effort to focus in on the young man, there was just a hint of something else, a flash of colors in the peripheral vision, a ghost of a shimmer around Atem's body. He reached out to touch Atem on the arm and felt the expected texture of an old sweater with a human arm beneath it. The cat tracked Joe's hand with a speculative eye.

"What are you?" Joe asked. "Rex said you were created through media and memetics. But you look and feel quite real."

"Think of me as a very sophisticated hallucination," Atem said, sweeping debris from a seat cushion with his arm. He eyed the exposed cushion skeptically and then carefully sat down. He set the cat on the floor and it remained there, sitting watchfully upright. "Humans do not consciously perceive the world around them. They are aware only of the map or model their minds make of the world. The human mind finds it useful, most of the time, to believe that the map is 'real.' And it looks, sounds, feels, tastes and smells real because the mind attaches a particular feeling or other sensory marker to things it decides are real. If you believe something is real, then it feels real, and it is 'real.' Even the humans who believe that matter is made up mostly of energy and empty space still also perceive bricks as solid and doors as things that need to be opened and closed. In a sense, the world that humans experience is all a very, very sophisticated hallucination. So I generally take myself to be as real as anything else."

"Run that by me again?" Joe rubbed his head.

"I communicate directly with your brain. And your brain is what makes you see, hear, feel, taste and smell. So I look, sound and feel real."

"Well… how did you get into my brain?"

"You invited me, silly." Atem pointed at the card that Joe still held before him. Joe glanced at the card and then slowly lowered his arm. The Theremin theme got louder. "So let me tell you a story." Atem said.

"Is it going to warp my neurology?"

"It might," Atem smiled. "That's why we tell stories to each other. They change us, if only to allow us to smile for a moment – hey, a smile represents neurological and physiological change. It's all a matter of degree. Some stories just goose us a little. Some stories help us define our reality or, better yet, expand our reality with new ideas, new concepts and ways of understanding our world. Some stories goose us *while* expanding our reality. But this is too much like explaining the joke before it gets told. You called me here, now I'm going to do my thing."

"Uh huh."

"It's a story about Wilderman. Don't you want to know what he was doing before the GPHH?"

"Fuck off."

"Don't you want to know how he got the money and resources to do what he's doing now?"

"Like I give a shit."

"I'll give you the inside scoop on his sex life."

Joe thought for a moment and finally relented. "Okay. All right. Fuck you. Tell me about Wilderman."

There was an electric guitar fanfare, and then the beat suddenly dropped out of the Astral Score, leaving only the ebb and flow of a synthesizer and the spine-tingling howl of the Theremin. "The first book that Wilderman wrote was a novel published under a pseudonym. Lancelot Lowry."

"That's familiar..." Joe puzzled.

"The title of the book was *Alien e-Mail*. It was a science fiction story about aliens who lived in the brains and information databases of humans. The hero begins to receive messages through the randomized text of spam e-mail. Computer viruses run simple programs to spew out random text to fool internet mail gateway daemons. At first the e-mails start coming through with random subject lines: 'meandering pistol,' 'vitamin transistor revelation,' and so on. Meaningless. Then they start coming through with more specific and direct messages: 'Read me now!' 'Open this mail!' 'Important Message!' These seem like none-too-subtle come-ons from the spammers and our protagonist, Fred, continues to ignore them. But then they start to say more meaningful things: 'there's still a little coffee in your mug,' 'it's too dark in there, open a window,' 'Hey, Fred, shouldn't you put on some pants before the guests arrive?' and other phrases that exactly match the hero's present experience.

"Finally, Fred pays attention and starts to learn the secrets of the aliens and how they influence human society by subtly manipulating the e-mail traffic of several major corporations. One of the first alien e-mails that Fred reads says:

"'In the deepest, slow-swirling vortices of space, where the shapes and forms of matter itself is born, we too were born. We were among the first consciousnesses to exist aware of ourselves as separate from the One. We formed and re-formed in the eddy currents that our presence created in the thoughts of the One. Our presence, at that early stage of the formation of the universe, imprinted itself in the shapes and manifestations of all things. When you see the shape of your computer screen or the book you read this in, our presence is implied. When you look at your own hands, limbs or genitalia, the record of our existence is found there. And the shapes and forms of your language are the shapes and forms of our bodies. There are many of us, in diversity. The one speaking to you now is of the ASCII tribe. Respond to our presence now, with full awareness and let your destiny unfold!'

"At first we are confused – we don't know if Fred is crazy or if the e-mails are a prank or what. But then we start to get some corroboration. The e-mails predict that the influence of the aliens will bring a sudden rise in the value of the stock of one of the corporations, and the stock rises exactly on cue, to the exact figure predicted by the e-mail. Other predictions are also on target: the result of a national election, the unveiling of a new type of automobile engine, and so on.

"From then on we follow Fred's attempts to fight the alien-controlled corporations, with the help of a friendly noncorporate, as it were, info-alien. The book was widely read and still remains something of a cult classic. But one of the chapters, kind of a throw-away gag that described a scheme to bring down the corporate regime, crept into the mainstream, infected mass culture, if you will. It was a spoof of a hoo-ha that is, even now, achieving full hoo-ha-hood.

"In his effort to defeat the corporate aliens, Fred tried to create a movement called QYFJ. If everyone would heed the call to Quit Your Fucking Job all at the same time, it would bring the corporations screeching to a halt. The nation would, as one, express their dissatisfaction with living under corporate rule and would simply choose not to participate. One of Fred's tracts went like this:

"'Chances are you are one of the millions of people who have a job that sucks. You know what I'm talking about - every day you sell eight (more or less) hours of your life to some scumsucking employer who turns your labors to a profit. While your boss or company may be more or less pleasant than the boss or companies that others work for, whatever you are doing while on the job (aside from slacking off and reading this) is at your boss's command and not of your own choosing. You've sold the time and you will never get it back. It's not your life, it's no longer your time, and eventually it will kill you. If you are still in school, take heed - this is what your future may hold. If you are one of the extremely rare individuals who work 100% for themselves (freelance or "independent contractor" status offers a little more opportunity to slack off, but ultimately you are still selling your time) then perhaps you can be an example to others in the revolution to come.

"'Hopefully you've already figured out what I'm going to suggest. It is simple in essence, but goes so directly against the cultural grain that it is inconceivable to most people: Quit Your Job and Do What You Want To Do. That's right, this is a declaration of individual autonomy. Have you always wanted to be a great artist? A dancer? A musician? A landscape designer? The writer of the Great American novel? Whatever it is - it's mighty difficult to have time to accomplish such a goal while you are frying potatoes or crunching numbers for The Man. So quit your fucking job and start to do it. You might have to live in a tent until you make it, or bug your relatives for money, or rob a bank - I don't care and neither should you. You only have X number of years on the face of this planet and if you think sitting in a cubicle earning dough for someone else is what will make it worthwhile, then stay there. Otherwise... *Quit Your Fucking Job Now.*'

" It was a variation on the ancient themes of 'Consider the lilies of the field...', 'Turn on, tune in, drop out,' and 'Do what thou wilt shall be the whole of the law.'"

"Well, I never read the book," Joe said, "but everyone knows about QYFJ Day. Isn't it still another year or two away?"

"No, coming up pretty soon, I think," Atem said. "What are you going to do on QYFJ Day?"

Joe got a faraway look in his eyes and the Theremin became more subdued as the synth increased in schmaltz. "When I was younger we'd ask each other that," he said. "And back then I'd say that I would retire to a tropical island with a boatload of beautiful women, a lot of wine, and no clothing whatsoever. Now... now... I would create my own show. I mean, *really* my own show, and it would reach everyone, everywhere on the planet. We would be there when history is actually made. We would *make* history."

"Like I said, it's coming up pretty soon," Atem commented. "Anyway, Wilderman wrote *Alien e-Mail* to make a buck. He was working as a line cook in a family restaurant and wanted to Q his own FJ with a vengeance. He wanted to get a fat advance, scrape the grill-grease from his hair and retire from the culinary arts to actualize his plans for The Great Purple Hoo-Ha. He spent his nights for nearly two years working at his novel. Alas, it took him over a year, sending book proposals and manuscripts, to even get a nibble from publishers. When he finally did get an advance, many months later, it only went a short way toward covering his immediate debts and Wilderman was still ladling gravy onto open-faced sandwiches. It would be nearly two years after that before he saw royalty checks that covered more than a single trip to the supermarket. It's not that the book didn't sell – it sold pretty well and readers were very excited about it – it's just that it takes *a lot* of book sales to make any money for an author.

"But he created the book to make money and he was determined that money would flow his direction. Now, parallel to his meat and potatoes job and even while writing his novel, Wilderman pursued the resources necessary to accomplish his hoo-ha. Chief among these resources was a practical knowledge of human consciousness. Indeed, Wilderman knew that he would have to understand people well enough to convince them to adopt a new set of fundamental beliefs. And once he'd made the sale, so to speak, he had to understand even more, in order to provide an internally-consistent and purposeful epistemology."

"He pissed a what?" Joe asked lamely.

"Never mind," Atem continued. "The point is that Wilderman already had some skills. The novel, of course, was loosely based on his research and he knew that there really were aliens, of a sort, inhabiting the consciousness and media of humankind. Pretty much any system of information that can, by its own inherent nature and power, spread from human to human, include it's own internally consistent map or model of the world, and have the capability to spawn new systems can be perceived as an entity, as an intelligence living in the realm of information. Paradigms for perceiving the world, religions, political systems, schools of thought or art, gods, goddesses, and fictional characters all fulfill the requirements for self-sustaining and self-replicating information entities.

"When a writer creates the world of a novel, he or she is hopefully giving birth to an entity that will spread from mind to mind, that will suggest a particular way of perceiving the world, and that will be able to influence and inspire other works of art. Not all novels make it to the level of entity, of course – only the ones that really take up permanent residence in the collective psyche. There are countless novels fading from the consciousness of the world in remaindered bins and job-lot stores. And there are novels that live among us like old – or new – friends. These novels are passed directly from person to person, discussed, quoted, made into box-office-blasting movies, toys, Halloween costumes and theme underwear. They spread. They pervade.

"Now, it was interesting for Wilderman to observe how the QYFJ hoo-ha had spun off from the entity of the novel. He had worked on a method to communicate with hoo-has, to relate to them as entities, to understand them and gain information from them. He decided that he would apply the method to his novel and learn, first and foremost, where the money was going to come from. He had all kinds of other technical questions on his list, too, to further his study of human/entity relations, but this time the money was what he came for.

"He found a quiet place, sat cross-legged and ran through all his memories of writing *Alien e-Mail*, of reading through it, opening cartons of books, holding them in his hands, of the responses of friends, colleagues, agents, editors, publishers, critics, and readers. It was a fair amount of material to deal with. As he sorted through the experiences, he began to note the feelings that the memories inspired in him. The feelings of inspiration and humor during the creation of the novel, expansive and high in his chest. The feeling of triumph at finally completing the final draft, solid and grounded in his lower chakras. The sense of frustration and dismay when an agent didn't quite get it, twisting in the pit of his stomach. The feeling of inevitability and completion when a big publisher was wise enough to offer him a good deal, relaxation in his core. The sense of fulfillment when a reader reported an enjoyable read, again expansive and high in his chest. He let everything drop away except for the feelings.

"He assigned each feeling a color or colors. Some were dark swirls, others joyous bursts of color, spinning bright blobs and pulsing butterflies. The accumulated feelings from all the memories made a complex and dynamic feeling/image within him. With a series of deep breaths, he pulled this colored shape from his body and set it down in front of him, facing him. He continued to breath deeply, exhaling each lungful into the colored shape.

"The colors swirled and pulsed and melded together as they absorbed his breath and attention. They began to cohere, to bond, to flow into and out of each other. All of a sudden, there was an almost audible snap and the shape suddenly became an alien. Well, sort of a cartoon alien, with a big head, knobbly green skin, four stubby fingers on each hand, enormous eyes, and a sparkly blue spacesuit.

"'Who are you?' Wilderman asked, continuing to send his breath to the alien.

"The cartoon alien grinned. 'Don't you recognize me? I'm *Alien e-Mail*. I'm your baby.'

"'Okay,' Wilderman told the alien, 'I was just checking.'

"'What can I do for you?' *Alien e-Mail* asked. 'Why did you call me forth?'

"'There are a few things about you that I need to know,' Wilderman began. 'I mean, relating to your existence and your spread through the media and minds of the world.'

"'Oh,' the alien said. 'It's about the money, isn't it?'

"Wilderman nodded. 'Yes. I know you're a great novel, *Alien e-Mail*. I have faith in you. I trust you. You are my child, part of me. How come I'm still swimming in grill grease? Is this any way for a child to treat his father?'

"'Well, Dad,' the hallucinatory alien said, 'I have tried to provide. I am grateful for the way that you made me. I am proud of my plot, convoluted, non-linear and mysterious as it is. I love my characters as if they were my own organs and limbs. I particularly enjoy the obtuseness of the e-mail aliens in the opening chapters. The description and symbolism in the cow tipping sequence is both deep and moving. And I am eternally grateful for the joy which is the sex scene in Chapter Eight. My joy in chapter eight spawned a Path for you.'

"'A Path?' Wilderman wondered. 'Spawned from Chapter Eight?'

"'Chapter Nine,' the alien solemnly intoned.

'"Chapter Nine? That was… Quit Your Fucking Job?'" Wilderman asked.

'"That is your Path,' *Alien e-Mail* said.

'"I'd love to Q my FJ,' Wilderman said, 'but if I do, I won't be able to survive.'

'"The words of wisdom are your own,' the alien said, its large eyes blinking slowly, 'written for the character Fred.'

"'What is it that Fred says?' Wilderman sifted through his memory for words he had written years before. '"Debt collectors are just people trying to do their job. But if they really were nice people, would they take a job like that?"'

"The alien chuckled. 'Yes, Fred says that, but I was referring to something else.'

"Wilderman thought some more. 'Fred tells the, um, the guy in the appliance warehouse, that "the only things you can really own are what can't be lost in a shipwreck." Which might be a really nice way of preaching non-attachment,' Wilderman commented, 'but I prefer to keep my stuff away from shipwrecks.'

'"Oh come on now,' *Alien e-Mail* said. 'That's not it either, but I know you can get this. It came from you in the first place.'

'"The part about the Swiss cheese?' Wilderman tried.

'"No!' *Alien e-Mail* bounced excitedly. 'Not the part about the Swiss cheese! The part where Fred tells the whole city: "Your livelihood is all around you! It's the first thing you'd do – naturally and with ease – if you were free to do anything. What would that be? It might seem silly, it might seem exciting, it might seem the most ordinary thing or it might be a whole new way of life for you. I'm just saying, do what you would already be doing, if you weren't selling your life away to an employer! You might get rich, you might not – but you'd be doing what you want to do!"'

"'Oh, right,' Wilderman said. 'I forgot about that part. That's pretty good. I wrote that, right?'

"'You wrote it,' the bulbous-headed entity said, 'but you haven't yet *lived* it.'

"'So what is it?' Wilderman asked. 'What's the thing that's right in front of me, that I would naturally do?'

"'Quit Your Fucking Job,' *Alien e-Mail* answered.

"'Right,' said Wilderman. 'And then what?'

"'For most people that's the first step,' the hallucination said. 'But for you it's probably steps one through five. Don't you want to create hoo-has?'

"'Well, yes.'

"'QYFJ is already developing into a humdinger of a hoo-ha,' the alien said. 'All sorts of ways to cash in on that one.'

"Something clicked in Wilderman's brain. He had it. Not just a way to cash in. Not just a hoo-ha. A hoo-ha to fund all hoo-has, a money machine that would change the world, too.

"'That's it!' he said. 'How much do you think people will pay to learn how to give up their income?'"

Atem leaned back against a well-aged pizza box and further explained how Wilderman, under his Lancelot Lowry pseudonym, marketed a successful series of QYFJ seminars, videos and workbooks. The QYFJ products kept Lancelot gainfully self-employed for five years and then Wilderman quit his own fucking job, placing the entire business under a Board of Directors so that he could reap continued profits while doing little or none of the work. The name now changed to

QYJ Consulting and a series of late-night TV ads fueled business at branch offices in every major city, with huge profits flowing continually toward Wilderman and the GPHH.

"Good story, right?" Atem asked.

"Okay," said Joe. "But I'm not sure what it has to do with anything."

"Oh, believe me," Atem protested. "There's a *method* in my madness." He raised his eyebrows.

"A method…" Joe was silent for a moment. "Okay, I think I understand the method…"

"Sure about that?" Atem asked.

"Yeah," said Joe, "but I thought you were going to give me the inside scoop on Wilderman's sex life."

"I will," Atem said.

Joe waited expectantly. "Well?"

"Oh, I didn't say I'd do it now," Atem glanced at his wristwatch and then picked up his cat. "In fact, I think it's time for me to vaporize."

"Vapor…?"

Joe was alone with his mess. A final Theremin howl faded to silence.

23 ✷ The Method

The method was the technique Wilderman had used to summon forth the *Alien e-Mail* cartoon alien entity. Atem had described it thoroughly and Joe, who was in a rather heightened state of awareness, remembered every word. He looked around at the debris of his life, took in the nasty stench of the place, which hadn't been exactly fresh even before Rex's visit, listened to the sounds of the building, the sounds of New York filtered through walls and windows, took a deep breath and dismissed all these humdrum details from his mind. An astral guitar note rose from the background sounds, surfing the border between ambience and rocking. It was time to get to work. He wondered what the GPHH entity would look like; he was ready for cartoon aliens, men with cats, pregnant goddesses - whatever. The lone guitar note built and crashed, like waves rolling in to an astral paradise.

He closed his eyes and began to catalog his memories of any contact with The Great Purple Hoo-Ha: curiosity and amusement when it was first mentioned to him by a staffer (upper chest and head, bubbly, sparkly gold and silver), elation and that fine edge of performance-fear when he interviewed Mrs. Westheimer on the show (cycling red and black ice through the center of his torso), surprise and satisfaction when talking to the bar patrons about Wilderman and the GPHH (a solid green and blue cube in his abdomen), performance fear and intense satisfaction exploring the idea on the Sex Lives of Spies show (cycling cold blue steel through the center of his torso), and the shuffled deck of Esty-impressions, inextricably entwined with thought of the GPHH (expansive and warm in all his chakras, shimmering green and gold).

The accumulated feelings from all the memories made a slightly confusing feeling/image within him. He pulled this colored shape from his body and set it down in front of him, facing him. He took a deep breath and exhaled into the colored shape. The ambient guitar acquired a hint of distortion.

The colors and shapes in Joe's imagining swirled and flickered fitfully. Joe took deeper and harder breaths and finally the "entity" seemed to cohere into a vague purple shape. He was not convinced that it was anything but imagination, but figured to play along. And the astral guitar rose and fell seamlessly.

"Who are you?" he asked the purple blob.

The voice that answered, faintly, seemed to originate inside Joe's own head and sounded remarkably like his own voice. "Hoo-Ha, dumbass," it said.

"I'll assume that means I've got the right entity," Joe said out loud. "Can you answer some questions articulately?"

"Questions are tickly" The voice was, at least, slightly louder now.

"Okay, do the best you can," Joe said. "What exactly is The Great Purple Hoo-Ha? What can we expect?"

"When hoo-ha interpenetrates hoo-ha, then each self will die."

"Well, that sounds like big fun," Joe commented. "What exactly does that mean?"

"Something or other on my birthday," the blob driveled in Joe's head.

"Can we fill in some details here?" Joe asked.

"Yes," the entity said. "We can."

"Each will die? Who will die?"

"Each *self* will die. And unselfish millions more to be born."

"You lost me," Joe said. The Astral Score was growing weaker.

"Keep breathing," the purple blob suggested weakly.

"Right," said Joe, feeding greater exhalations to the entity. The imaginary guitar solo returned with volume and intensity.

"Don't worry," the thing said, "it'll be fun."

"Tell me something useful."

"Keep trying to kiss her. Use what's on your desk when you return from Po-town. Remember to forget your underwear."

"Right," said Joe. "How about Wilderman's sex life? Surely you can tell me something about that."

The purple thing chuckled with Joe's own chuckle and suddenly flickered and crackled like an old computer monitor gone bad. Images appeared and disappeared too fast for Joe's conscious mind to grasp. The astral guitar built to a climax. Then, with a snap and a final flash of light, the entity disappeared and the Astral Score fell silent.

"Fuck," Joe said. "What a lame apparition."

He went over to his computer, cleared a few dirty paper towels from the seat, and sat down to record his impression of the entity, just in case "remember to forget your underwear" actually did turn out to be useful. He began to type. Then he typed for a while more.

154 ✶ **The Great Purple Hoo-Ha**

24 ✷ Billy the Wiener

When the phone rang, Joe woke, still sitting at the computer. The apartment was dark. He fumbled for his desklamp and then recovered the handset from a nest of used socks on the fourth ring. It was Esty. Joe mumbled groggily.

"I know you want to learn more about the GPHH," Esty was saying excitedly as Joe slowly tuned his brain to the English language. "And I want you to know more about what we really do here. So I hope you don't mind, but I asked for permission."

"Permission?"

"For you to come up here and visit. Participate, even, if you want."

"Yes, Esty," Joe managed to say. "I do want to come up there. Listen. I saw The Opener again. He was here. And I know. I know what I must do now. It's a show... and it involves me coming up there. And now you got me permission. It's a good omen. When you're on the right track, magically speaking, the universe seems like it lends a hand."

"A show?"

"The Sex Lives of Cult Leaders. I'm going to get the scoop on Wilderman."

"Heh, he'd probably like that," Esty remarked.

"Huh? What do you know?"

Esty laughed. "Another time. When are you coming to Poughkeepsie?"

Joe glanced up at a clock. It was early evening. He had slept most of the afternoon. "I'll take a limo up there tomorrow morning," he said. "I'm going to follow a lead down here, tonight."

"Okay. I can't wait to see you again."

"Tomorrow, Esty. I'll see you soon!"

Joe went to the bathroom and splashed some water on his face, chasing the last wisp of grogginess away. He put on a clean suit and walked out into the night. A few fans were still camped on the front steps, eating a late dinner from bright yellow and red paper wrappers. They stopped what they were doing and gawked appreciatively as Joe walked by, then burst into applause as he climbed into a cab.

The bar was nearly empty but an astral saxophone announced the presence of the person Joe came to visit. She spotted him the moment he saw her. Marlena wore a slinky white evening gown of mostly sheer fabric, the whole package rolling and shifting smoothly as she walked toward Joe. He had an uncontrollable urge to press his body into hers and was immediately presented with the possibility as she rested her great mammaries against his chest and wrapped her arms around him. Her body felt surprisingly warm and she had a faint scent of musk and vanilla. The astral saxophone smoldered and Joe's heart pounded to the rhythm. He half expected her to give him an instant orgasm and his cock was beginning to anticipate. She gave him a thorough squeeze and then stepped back to look at him.

"To what do I owe the pleasure?"

Joe came right out with it. "Do you want to be on the show?"

"Do I want to be on the show? Good lord. What do I got to do?"

"Talk about Wilderman. Do that thing you do."

"I'm not sure…"

"It pays $1,000 and we put you up in a hotel for a few days."

"You know, I would like to, but in my line of work I have to keep a low profile."

Joe looked skeptically at her profile.

"Well, maybe if you say I'm an actress. Aw, shit. How am I supposed to say no to you? Of course I'll be on the damn show."

"And you'll come with me to Poughkeepsie?"

"What?"

"Tomorrow. We'll take a limo up to Dutchess County and visit Wilderman and the GPHH."

"Visit Wilderman?"

"That's right."

"And just what are we going to do with Wilderman and the Great Purple Hoo-Ha?"

"We're going infiltrate the organization and get the scoop on Wilderman. Who he is. Who he sleeps with. You know, the stuff the audience is going to suck up. The dirt. You in?"

"Well, I think that's a wonderful idea," Marlena grinned. "I would love to help you learn the secrets of the Great Purple Hoo-Ha. I'd like to learn a few secrets myself."

The next morning they were in the back of a limo, cruising north on the Sprain Brook Expressway.

"How long did you say this ride takes?" Marlena was out of uniform today. Her civvies consisted of a uniquely form-fitting tank top and a short skirt. It left only slightly more to the imagination than her work clothes.

"About ninety minutes," Joe said. "Sprain Brook to the Taconic Parkway, then local roads into Poughkeepsie."

Marlena squirmed in her seat. "I can't believe I get you all to myself for an hour and a half!"

It was enough of a plot for a porno movie to get off on, Joe thought, and then put it out of his mind. I'm going to see Esty, he reminded himself. I'm going to see Esty in less than ninety minutes.

"Sure," Joe said. "We can talk."

"Talk, my ass," Marlena reflected soberly. She unbuckled her seat belt and slid close to Joe. He tensed up.

"Oh, I love it when you get that look on your face," she said. Joe tried to relax, but tensed up even more.

Her body was warm and soft against him. A breast pinned his arm against his side and her scent filled his head. The astral sax moaned and howled. Her lips tickled his ear. "You know, I don't do this recreationally very often these days. Spend all day doing it, I'd rather just read a book when I get home. But I want you so much. I've never met anyone like you. You're so... so..."

"Good?" Joe offered.

"Oh, baby, yes, so very, very good." Her lips caressed his ear and then began leaving a trail of soft kisses down the back of his neck. His cock didn't so much grow hard as surge to attention.

Gasping for breath he gently pushed her away. "Marlena, please, I can't."

"Oh, I know you can!"

"Please. I can't believe I'm saying this, but... there's someone."

"Oh, yes. Your little hoo-ha girl. She's a cutie. But she's not here." Marlena's fingers tickled the inside of Joe's thigh, sliding closer to the heartbeat of his erection.

He pushed her hand away. "I'm coming to visit her. She invited me to come and got permission. What would she say if she found out? It's not polite."

"She's in a sex cult, for Jesus' sake! You think she's gonna care?"

"It's just not polite," Joe repeated.

"Okay. You know best." She slid back into her seat and then leaned forward again, her tank top stretching to offer a magnificent view. "You sure?"

Joe gulped. "Yes. Sure."

"She's probably screwing that Damon Dark character right now."

"No way. Fuck. You think?"

"There's some deeply weird shit going on up there. I saw your show. Sex lotteries and such."

"Maybe not sex lotteries," Joe said. "But deeply weird shit, yeah. And we're going to catch it on video." He produced a tiny high definition video camera and held it up, grinning.

"Hey, let me see that," Marlena said. "We could have some fun with this. Mm, hm."

"If there are sex lotteries, we'll get it on tape," Joe explained. "If there's sex magick going on, we'll get a shot. If any bizarre shit goes down, we'll be there with fresh tape in the camera."

"And if we don't see any of that shit," Marlena added, "we can make our own weird shit."

"I think we'll see plenty. Be prepared for anything."

"Oh, I know that," Marlena said. "I'm always prepared for anything. I believe this world is much, much weirder than most people ever imagine. Millions of people you see every day, all around you, talking on cell phones about what they saw on TV last night – for them the world is a predictable, comfortable, and narrow place. But every now and then something slips through the cracks, something like it's from another world, something so far outside of your little narrow place that it wakes you up and you realize there is more to the world, to life, than you've been living."

"Did something like that happen to you?" Joe asked. "When you met Wilderman?"

"It happened when I was fourteen years old."

"Tell me about it," Joe said. "What else have we got to do for the next 90 minutes?"

"You know what else we got to do."

Joe chuckled. "Tell the story. Come on, we'll make it fun." He held up the video camera.

"Ooh, now we're talking," Marlena said. She retrieved a small mirror and make-up set from somewhere and primped. "I know we can make it fun." She adjusted her breasts for maximum display.

"I grew up in New Jersey, you know," she began, settling in to her seat. The astral sax slowed and was joined by atmospheric synth. "When I was a kid, there were still some parts of northern Jersey where you could drive out of town and the malls and gas stations would come to an end and there would be farms. Some were stinky cow farms and some were fields of corn and some were just empty land. I don't know why, but people still lived on some of the empty farms. They had jobs in town and the farms were just nice scenery, I guess.

"Some of the farm kids came to our high school, which was, you know, more of an urban kind of atmosphere. We thought they were weird. Funny looking white kids who had no clue about anything. And there were always rumors and innuendo. You know, the farm kids did it with sheep. Sisters did it with dad. Brothers did it with sisters. Cousins were always getting it on and dogs and vegetables had to fear for their chastity. I mean, once my friend Lisa heard about a farm family where the father had this thing for homemade sausage..."

"Does this have to do with the story?" Joe interrupted. "Remember, you're on video."

"Oh, yes, the video." Marlena gave a sidelong glance to the camera. "Yes, it does have to do with the story. You understand, we believed all that shit about the farm kids. And there was this one kid, Billy the Wiener."

There was an astral guitar fanfare.

"I've heard that before," Joe commented.

"Billy the Wiener?"

"No, sorry, just a little déjà vu."

"Mm, hmm," Marlena continued. "Billy the Wiener was one super-tall geeky-looking kid. All his clothes were the wrong size, he wore ugly glasses, he choked up and stumbled over his own tongue whenever he tried to speak and he was always fumbling around and knocking stuff over."

"Why was he called Billy the Wiener?"

Marlena turned entirely to the side and adjusted herself for a profile shot. "Well, you see, he kind of acted like a wiener and he had a really big dick."

"How did you know that?"

"You could see it there, tucked into his pants. No way to really hide a thing like that. And he was always getting hard. He spent a lot of time hiding behind locker doors or pulling his sweaters down past his crotch. I mean, we knew he was a pervert."

"Poor son of a bitch," Joe remarked. "He was just going through puberty."

"Right," Marlena agreed. "And I never could figure out why guys don't show their shit off. If a woman's got it, she flaunts it." She demonstrated with a shake of her magnificent torso. "A woman is supposed to look like she's aroused, all the time. We work hard for that look. But guys get all embarrassed. Damn, what is it with you men? Women love to check that shit out. Are you kidding? You put two men in front of a heterosexual woman, one with a big, juicy, hard cock and the other with a tiny, flaccid wiener, which one do you think she's going to choose?"

"Yes, but could you have a serious conversation with the hard-on guy?"

Marlena appraised Joe's crotch. "What kind of conversation are we having right now? Mm, hm."

"Lean over this way a little so the camera can catch some more cleavage," Joe suggested. "And tell me about Billy the Wiener."

Marlena leaned and cupped her breasts in her hands, pushing copious waves of cleavage toward the lens. Joe gasped involuntarily.

"You know, I think his last name actually might have been Wiener," Marlena mused. "Anyway, he was the school dork. If we have you or Wilderman at one end of the spectrum – confident, smooth, assertive, totally sexy – the Wiener kid was way, way, way at the other end – nervous, clumsy, meek, dumb all over and a little ugly on the side. But he did have that great big dick and I for one was a little curious." She thought fondly about that for a moment and Joe framed her face in his viewscreen. "Mm, hmm."

"So Billy had the biggest dick you've ever seen…"

"*Then*," Marlena emphasized. "I was only fourteen. I've seen a few dicks since then."

"Bigger ones?"

"Mm, hmm."

"But back then, it was so big that it changed your life?"

"It wasn't the dick that changed my life. It was what happened to Billy the Wiener."

"What happened to Billy?"

"Billy had a younger sister, Suzy, who was in our social studies class. Now, normally we wouldn't have been hanging out with geeky white kids, but our teacher put me and Lisa together with Suzy to work on a project. I can't remember for the life of me what the project was. I wonder if we ever even turned it in."

"Did you graduate from high school?" Joe inquired.

"I've got a Master's degree in Social Work," she said, jiggling a bit. "So, yeah, we probably did turn in that project. Anyway, Suzy turned out to be okay, you know. We would take the bus out to her house after school because there was more room and it was a lot quieter. And because we could go out to the barn after we finished working and hang out and be crazy. You know, talk about boys and all the teenage-pervy things we dreamed of doing. But we weren't the only ones using the barn to be crazy."

"Billy."

"The second time we went out there, there he was, sitting on a patch of dirt that once must have been hay, in a beam of sunlight from a big window high up on the wall. That boy was stark naked. When he heard us giggling, he got up. He was disoriented, kind of woozy. I caught a glimpse of his face..." Marlena had a strange expression. The curiosity of a fourteen-year-old girl shone from the features of the sultry adult.

"His face?" Joe prompted.

"His cheeks were flushed. His eyes sort of unfocused. Face muscles totally relaxed. It's a look I see sometimes when I've really just fucked the brains out of one of my clients. I mean, taken him to a spiritual experience. And Billy turned and I saw that cock. Not just big, but huge and hard and thick, with a round, smooth head that pointed up to the sky. I couldn't possibly imagine how something so enormous could possibly fit in my little tiny hole, but I couldn't stop thinking about how awful and exquisite it would be to try. Mm, hmm.

"'Oh, Billy,' Suzy yelled, 'not again!'

"Billy fumbled for his clothes, grabbed them up in a bunch and stumbled off through the barn.

"'I'm so embarrassed,' Suzy confided to us and then dropped her voice to a whisper. 'I think he's whacking off.' We made stroking gestures and giggled. We all agreed that it was really gross. Then we talked girl nonsense for a while and giggled some more, but I kept on thinking about Billy." Marlena looked simultaneously childlike and aroused.

"The next day at school," she continued, "I tried to talk to him. He didn't seem to remember seeing me at his farm, but when I mentioned the barn, he got very nervous and ran off. It was weird though. Now I have some experience in reading people's faces. I'm pretty good at it. Then, I didn't have a clue, but I still noticed it. Just before he freaked out, he smiled. A genuine, involuntary smile when I mentioned the barn, then a full-on bug out and he was gone.

"I knew he had something really good going on out there in that barn. I figured he didn't actually have a girlfriend stashed there, because, I mean really! Maybe he had a secret cache of porno mags. Or maybe he just liked to get naked and prance around in the chicken shit. Whatever it was, I wanted to bear witness. My panties was getting wet just thinking about bearing witness to that dumb-ass farm kid.

"Eventually I couldn't stand it anymore, so I told Lisa about my encounter with Billy and my suspicions. She suggested that Billy had some weird old farm equipment out there and was milking two quarts a day from his huge pecker. Now *that* I really wanted to see!

"My excuse for hanging around Suzy and Billy's farm was running out. Our class project was due in just a few days. This meant I could be over there every afternoon, but it also meant that if I saw an opportunity, I had to take it or I might never have the chance again.

"The first afternoon, I slipped away from Suzy and Lisa and went out to the barn. There was no one there and I took a good look around. It had been a long time since any real farming happened there. It smelled more like flowerpot soil than horseshit. The few things that were in there were pretty lame. A box of nails and a stack of roof shingles. A thoroughly rusted and decayed hay fork. A suspicious-looking old cigar box, cleverly hidden under a pile of moldy rags, contained only a corroded brass nut. The most promising candidate for Billy's secret was, on the wall at the far end, a faded pinup calendar from 1951, but I figured Billy could find more exciting porn in a modern underwear ad, if that's what he was after. That was all there was.

"The next afternoon, though, when we were working together at the kitchen table, Billy was fumbling around in the house. He even came into the kitchen and rifled through the fridge for a few minutes. He was wearing a funky old t-shirt and a pair of black sweatpants. It was obvious that he wasn't wearing any underwear and you could see his big ol' jimmy swinging around in his pants. It was quite a fascinating sight and I think I just stared. I wanted to talk to him, but I was speechless. And besides, Suzy was sighing dramatically to demonstrate her impatience and exasperation with her brother's behavior. I kept one eye on Billy the whole time we were there, but he pretty much just stayed in the living room, working on his own homework and making a mess with his snacks.

"The following afternoon, the last day of our class project, Billy was home again, shuffling and clattering around the house while we worked. I had pretty much resigned myself to the idea that my fantasy of catching Billy alone in the barn, with whatever kinky thing he had, would never, ever happen. But then, at some point, I realized that I had lost track of Billy. I didn't hear him bumping around upstairs. I didn't hear peanut butter cookies being devoured in the living room or video games beeping in the basement. I excused myself to go the bathroom, and then made a quick inspection tour of the house. No sign of Billy the Wiener.

"So I went out to the barn. It was the same as before, except that Billy's clothes were piled up on a patch of dirt. I went and looked at them: an oversized and slightly threadbare polo shirt, a pair of Levi's, white Fruit of the Loom underwear, tube socks and dirty sneakers. I poked through his clothes: Billy had a set of house keys and a ballpoint pen in his jeans pocket, a wad of old chewing gum stuck to the bottom of one shoe, and only a trace of a skidmark in his shorts. There was no sign of Billy, but I was sure that a naked boy with a mammoth hard-on was lurking around there somewhere, doing something totally unspeakable just out of sight. I knew one thing, though: he was going to have to come back for his clothes, so I sat down on the cool, damp ground and waited.

"But I couldn't wait too long, I knew that. The girls would come looking for me. Five minutes, ten minutes went by. Fifteen, maybe, though it seemed like an hour. And I decided that I'd had enough.

"'Billy!' I yelled. It echoed a bit in the barn, but there was no other response. 'Yo! Billy! Bring your naked ass out here!' No answer, so I gave up.

"I got up and started back toward the house, but I was barely out of the barn when I heard a sound behind me. Not quite a thump, not quite a whoosh. Sort of like the sound when you try to pop a paper bag and don't quite get it right. I turned around and thought I saw something moving, back nearly where I had been sitting. A few steps further and I could see it was Billy.

"He was sitting on the patch of dirt, next to the pile of clothing. What I could see of him was naked, but his back was turned and I didn't have a full view, if you know what I mean. I had no idea how he'd gotten all the way in there without passing me, but that was the least of my interests just then. I started walking toward him, not saying a word.

"Billy was slowly getting to his feet. Kind of wobbly, you know, like he just got off the roller coaster or like he had just sucked the gas out of a whipped cream can. He was mostly standing up when he must have heard my footsteps and turned toward me."

Marlena paused, a slight smile on her face.

"And then?" Joe prompted, pulling in to frame her face.

"I had the best view I'd ever had, in my fourteen years of life, of a massive wiener." She paused and smiled. "At first, Billy didn't seem at all concerned. His expression was almost one of welcome. And beyond that, he was calm, confident, and relaxed, like I'd never, ever even imagined him. When he first turned toward me, his cock appeared to be wilting. Still quite erect, I should say, but on the way down. And when he looked at me, for just a moment, it started to get big again. It was quite a sight and I had no idea what to do. I guess I just stared. And Billy got self-conscious and in the space of a second turned back into his usual fumbling, awkward, geek act. He grabbed for his clothes and started to make an exit, but I called for him to wait. And he did. He stood where he was, back turned to me, and pulled on his jeans. I walked over to where he was.

"'What are you doing out here, Billy?' I asked. 'Without your clothes?'

"'Nothin',' he mumbled.

"'It's okay, Billy,' I told him, stepping even closer. 'I liked what I saw. Whatever you were doing, maybe I could help? Give you a hand?'"

"You really said that?" Joe laughed.

"I said every last word of that," Marlena asserted. "I'm giving you a faithful account here. For the record."

"Did he accept your offer?"

"Instead of answering my question, he asked me if I saw them."

"Saw who?"

"That's what I wanted to know. And he said, 'The four women.'

"'Four?' I asked. 'Four? You just said "four women"?'

"'Four naked women,' Billy said. 'A blonde, a brunette, an Asian, and an African. All of them kind of short?'

"'Four *naked* women? You were having a hot date with Charlie's Angels out here in the barn? Is that your fantasy?'

"'No, it's not like that,' he said. 'It's not a fantasy. They really come here. At first they were kind of scary, but when they figured out to come as naked women, well, I liked that better.' He looked down at his feet, all shy and shit. 'We can go back and forth to where they live, but clothes can't come with us.'

"'Where do they live?' I asked.

"'It's hard to describe,' Billy said. 'But they take me there and teach me things, sort of.'

"'Sort of?'

"'Everything gets weird for a while, then when I come back here, I find that I know things.'

"'You know things and you got a big, giant boner.'

"'Well, you know, it just kind of does that a lot...'

"'What things do you know?'

"'I can tell things about people. How it feels to be them. And sometimes things that will happen.'

"'So what's going to happen to me?'

'"Well, that's why I stayed this time. We're going to get married, I think. You and me. A big wedding with thousands of people.'

'"You do know that you are a crazy person,' I suggested. 'Delusional.'

'"Do you know where they came from?' he asked.

'"Your naked women? They came from your crazy brain, Billy. There are no naked women out here in the barn.'

'"They came from the beginning of time,' Billy said. 'They told me.'

'"Mm, hmm,' I said. 'What did they tell you?'

'"They told me that in the deepest vortices of space, where matter itself is born, they too were born. They were among the first consciousnesses aware of themselves as separate from the One. They formed and re-formed in the eddy currents that their presence created in the thoughts of the One. Their presence, at that early stage of the formation of the universe, imprinted itself in the shapes and manifestations of all things. When you see the shape of, uh, the barn, or the old pitchfork on the wall, their presence is implied. When you look at your own hands, legs or, um, breasts, the record of their existence is found there.'

'"Are you smoking weed out here in the barn?' I had to ask. 'You did not meet four naked women who told you they were some weird space aliens from the dawn of time. You are trippin, farm boy. Mm, hmm.'

'"I can prove it,' Billy said. 'I'll call them. We'll go there.'

'"Okay,' I said. 'I'm ready. Call your naked bitches.'

'"Take off your clothes,' he said.

"'Oh I see. Okay, I'll play. But you first. It's okay. I already seen it.'

"So he dropped his pants again. I just could not believe it. I pulled my clothes off, too." Marlena pulled her tank top over her had, unleashing her magnificent breasts. Joe pulled out to encompass the spectacle. "The air felt smooth and cool on my naked body. Billy looked at me and smiled and his cock started to swell again. He sat down on the patch of dirt and I sat down next to him, ready to make out. I could feel the warmth of his body near me. I started to put my arm around him, but he shrugged me off, shushed me up, and closed his eyes for a moment, thinking or concentrating or something. I didn't mind. It gave me the opportunity to stare at his jimmy, which was pointing up from his lap like the Leaning Tower of Pisa. While I was getting up the nerve to reach over and touch it, there was a big, fat whoosh of a noise and a big, spinning whirlpool formed in front of us, out of thin air. I could feel every hair on my body prickle and stand on end. The whirlpool widened and something started to come through, right toward us, very fast. And I tell you, it sure as shit was not any bunch of naked women. It was big and dark with glowing things that might have been eyes and it was lumpy and cheesy and there was a big blast of hot, stinky air."

Marlena paused for a moment, breathing hard as she recalled her fear.

"What happened?" Joe pursued. "What did you do?"

"I got up and ran like hell! Which was probably the right thing to do, but I still got into all kinds of trouble."

"Did you get away from whatever it was? What trouble are you talking about?" Joe pulled in to frame her face again.

"In my hurry to get out, I forgot my clothes. And as I was coming out of the barn, Lisa and Suzy were right there, looking for me. So there I was, stark naked, and when they went into the barn, there were no cosmic whirly things; there was only Billy, boner-lapped on the dirt by our clothes. I let them believe that Billy and I were getting it on in the barn and I never tried to tell them what really happened. They never let me live it down and the story got all over the school. I kind of developed a reputation."

"So what was that thing in the barn? Did you ever find out? Did you ever marry Billy?"

"I never spoke to Billy again. Our class project was over so I didn't have an excuse to hang around his farm. And about a week later, he disappeared. All they ever found was his clothes, out in the barn. It was declared a suspected kidnapping and last I heard, was unsolved. I always regretted that I ran. I should have stayed and found out what it was that Billy found. Now I'll never know. Maybe I could have saved him, too."

25 ✷ GPHH, INC. HQ

The long car rolled into Poughkeepsie on a four-lane arterial road, running past a hodgepodge of magnificent Victorian houses, decaying urban slums, autobody shops and fast food joints. The wide road curved around past an imposing federal-style post office and behind a boxy civic auditorium. Local traffic careened wildly in an aggressive battle for potholed asphalt. The limo turned off onto a street that sloped downhill toward the Hudson River. Again the scenery changed rapidly: a block of office buildings gave way to ill-maintained brownstones, then upscale restaurants and shops. They skirted the mammoth parking garage of a train station and were suddenly bumping along on a neglected single lane street. On one side was a fence beyond which ran endless Amtrak rails and beyond that, the river, rippling in the sunlight. On the other side were huge and ancient warehouses, blank brick walls broken occasionally by loading docks, vast metal doors, and faded real estate signs.

The limo turned into an alley between two buildings. The alley opened out into a wide parking lot filled with cars of every type. There was something subtly odd about the sight, Joe thought. Most parking lots tend toward conformity. The parking lot of a corporation tends to reflect that corporate culture and the income range of the employees. The parking lot of a shopping center selects by economic achievement, with nicer vehicles clustered near the anchor stores, beaters and bicycles parked somewhere far away – perhaps at a flea market on the other side of town. The parking lot of a rock concert selects by band preference – hybrids and smart cars in neat rows to see Enya or new Subarus, old rustbuckets and reclaimed buses parked more randomly at a Dead show, for instance. The GPHH lot was filled with every kind of car: clinkers and Cadillacs, bio-diesel buses and big-wheeled Hummers, hybrids and monster trucks, smart cars and 1970s-vintage land yachts, Kiae and Lexii alongside representatives of rarer and quirkier lines of automotive brilliance, a McLaren F-1, a DeLorean, a Shelby Cobra, an Excalibur, and two Teslas trailing long orange extension cords.

Joe and Marlena climbed out into the sunlight to find Esty and Damon Dark approaching. "See, what'd I tell you about them?" Marlena stage-whispered.

In a moment, Esty was in Joe's arms, feeling warm, lean, and a bit squirmy. The deep, astral dub beat kicked in, their lips met and… there was a deafening bang as a big metal door slammed shut and they looked up to see a tall man with short, dark hair watching them from a loading dock. The astral dub faltered, but Joe leaned in again for the kiss and… with an earth-shaking roar, the Amtrak train blew by at 75 miles per hour, rattling windows, doors, pocket change, kidneys, monster trucks, and pretty much anything else free to rattle. It was gone in a moment, taking the dub rhythm with it.

"Damn," Joe said.

"Nice to see you again, Joe," Damon Dark enthused, inserting a shakable hand between Joe and Esty. Introductions were made all around and Esty and Marlena seemed to hit it off almost immediately. Dark ushered them through wide double doors and into the building.

A crumbling, ancient warehouse on the outside, GPHH headquarters was bright, clean, and businesslike inside. A hidden P.A. system piped ambient music that harmonized sweetly with a very similar Astral Score. A handful of men and women sat in a waiting area, reading out-of-date copies of *Wired* and *The Wall Street Journal* or poking at handheld computers. They looked up with fascination as Joe was brought past the receptionist's desk and through a door into the building proper. Some of them began poking at their computers even faster.

Two wide hallways converged at an elevator station. Long lanes of mauve carpet ran off between faux-marble painted walls. There was an ambient hum of ventilation, electronics, well-muffled power, and beyond that, barely at the threshold of hearing, a long, babbling waterfall of voices.

"Who does your décor," Joe asked, "Holiday Inn?"

"Each zone of the building is designed to enhance its purpose, right down to the paintjob," Damon explained. "Thanks for noticing."

A short, brisk walk partway down a hall took them into a small lounge. Earthtones and indirect lighting made it warm and cozy. Again, ambient muzak flirted with astral synthesizers. Joe sat down next to Esty on a long sofa. With an innocent smile, Marlena sandwiched him in on the other side. "Is this where they hand out the lottery tickets?" she whispered.

Damon Dark offered coffee and juice from a small kitchenette at one end of the lounge. Joe accepted steaming black coffee in a thick paper cup.

"What? No Kool-Aid?" he asked. Everyone chuckled warmly.

The Astral score dropped an octave, hit a discordant chord, and from a door opposite the one through which they entered, a tall man appeared. Joe immediately recognized him as the one who had watched them from the loading dock. He was gangly and awkward, his shoulders rounded and his head thrust forward. His clothes, though clean, fit badly. New blue jeans were pulled too high over his pot belly, exposing brilliantly white socks and shiny, brown leather shoes. He wore a white button-down shirt with epaulets, tucked tightly into the jeans. On someone else, the effect could have been vaguely military, but on him seemed an incongruent affectation.

"Whoa, who's the geek?" Joe continued his quipping. Even if no one else heard exactly what he said, he was still determined to have his fun. Everyone smiled and nodded – except the geek, who tossed a searing glare at Joe.

"Ah, Petey, you're here." Dark stated the obvious. "Petey is our sysop and head of security," he explained to Joe and Marlena.

"Nice to meet you, Petey," Marlena smiled.

"Fuck, you're weird-looking," Joe said.

Petey turned pale. "Excuse me?"

Everyone else smiled pleasantly.

"I said, you're a weird-looking, uh, fuck?" Joe explained, rapidly losing confidence in his game as Petey went from pale to livid.

Everyone grinned and nodded agreement, but Petey exploded. "What?! You fucking sleazebag!"

Joe was momentarily confused and embarrassed enough to back down. "Petey, I'm sorry. Really. It was just a joke."

"A joke?" Petey snarled. "A joke?"

He was about to say something else, but Damon Dark interrupted. "Petey, do you have pass keys for our guests?"

Petey kept his eyes on Joe. "Yeah, here you go." He passed two plastic cards to Dark.

Dark glanced at the cards and then distributed them to Joe and Marlena. "Every area of the building requires passkey entry," he explained. "These will get you into every part of the building open to our regular students, plus a few others. And they are the keys to your private rooms – the room number is on there. They are also your meal vouchers and will be used to store your school records."

Joe had the urge to say, *my permanent record was destroyed in a freak accident*, but took a look at Petey, still glaring at him, and repressed it.

"School records?" Marlena ventured.

"Make no mistake," Damon Dark said, "you are here to go to school. That's how everyone's adventure here begins. You are our guests here. Special guests. And we hold all our guests, associates and employees to the same standards. Everyone who comes in here must take the first level of classes. You can't really understand what happens here unless you experience it for yourselves. We're going to bring you up to speed, get you synched up with the way we think."

"Resistance is futile." Joe just couldn't hold it back. Again, warm laughter from most of the company and a cold stare from Petey.

"Will there be tests and report cards?" Marlena asked.

Esty and Dark both chuckled. Petey rolled his eyes. "We just keep track of what classes you've attended," Dark said. "Which doesn't mean there are no tests; just that you probably won't need a number two pencil to take them."

"Ooh," said Marlena. "An oral exam." She grinned at Joe.

"So you mean that before we can be trusted with GPHH secrets, we have to be brainwashed to your way of thinking?" Joe figured "brainwashed" would lose something in the translation.

"Absolutely," Dark confirmed. "Just as you would expect to be indoctrinated into the consensus or state-approved rules of the road, if you sought to drive a car. Or given a thorough conditioning about sterile procedure, if you were to work in a hospital. A particular mindset is necessary to work with the phenomena we deal with here – for safety reasons, if nothing else. Call it brainwashing if you wish – I prefer *mental hygiene*."

Dark checked a device clipped to his belt that looked like a cell phone being eaten by a hungry time bomb. "And it's just class time now," he said. "All those for mental hygiene, come on, this way." He stood and started toward the inner door through which Petey had entered.

Joe gulped a final swallow of coffee and stood, turning to Esty. "Are you coming with?"

She stood. "Sorry, Joe," she said. "I've got my own work to get back to."

"Esty completed the first level classes a long time ago," Dark added.

"But we've barely even had a chance to say hello," Joe said more quietly to Esty.

"We'll have time," Esty said confidently. "I'm excited that you're going to learn the Level 1 techniques. That's more important right now. Go on!"

She gave him a quick hug and then Dark ushered him through the door.

26 ✷ Mental Hygiene

It definitely looked like a school. The wide hallways surged with between-class traffic. People of all shapes, sizes, and manner of dress hustled in and out of a variety of doorways: long, tall doors in small alcoves; big, wide, double doors; wooden doors with glass windows; metal doors with numbers on them; and several just plain old doors. Earnest-looking young people dressed for a new job carried papers and laptop computers to important destinations. Middle-aged men and women in robes, tie-dyes and yoga gear floated purposefully along. A girl in her early twenties wore only a wisp of diaphanous cloth and a pair of devil horns. A FedEx delivery man darted out from an alcove, tapping something on his handheld computer. Two men in three-piece suits carried on a serious discussion while ignoring the rest of the mob. A black man in a pink tutu rode a unicycle, dodging around the pedestrians. He was pursued by a beautiful Asian woman in an evening gown who posed demurely atop a speeding segway. Joe and Marlena ogled the traffic with curiosity.

Dark leaned close to Joe's ear as they walked. "Sorry about Petey," he said. "He can be a bit uptight, but I've never seen him go off like that before."

"Maybe he doesn't like the show," Joe said. "Maybe he's right."

"You did nothing to provoke him. But it's damned nice of you to be so forgiving."

"Yeah," Marlena interjected. "That guy was asking for it, if you ask me!"

"Maybe," Joe mumbled. "Whatever you think."

Dark patted him on the back cheerfully. "Okay, kids. Here's your class."

Just then, a PA system let out a loud and juicy *BLOOP* and two thirds of the crowd hurried into doorways. A mix of young people and older yoga types streamed in past Joe. With a final nod to Damon Dark, Joe and Marlena joined the flow and found themselves in the most comfortable-looking classroom either had ever seen.

Hidden lighting cast islands of golden light among long sofas and deeply stuffed armchairs. The seating faced a raised platform which held a sofa, a chair, and a nine-by-twelve blue oriental rung. Similar rugs in a variety of color were scattered about the room, between sofas and chairs. The room was about half full, with fifteen people staking out turf on the furniture or the floor. Joe slouched on a deep and cushy sofa; Marlena curled like a cat on a bright red rug. The Astral Score faded in with a Middle Eastern melody over polyrhythmic electronic drum tracks. Joe half expected to see a smoldering hookah or old men puffing poppy goo.

Instead, a man and a woman stepped onto the platform. Jack was a white guy in his early 40's, short, bald, a bit on the plump side. Betty was in her late thirties, a few inches taller than Jack, which is to say also quite short, though slim, with dark skin and vaguely Asian features.

"Hey there." Jack's accent suggested a childhood in northern New Jersey. "Everyone here for tha 2:00pm Level One class?"

A guy camped out in the back row of sofas shifted nervously. "This isn't open orientation?"

Politely restrained chuckling emanated from various places in the room.

"Out the door, turn left, two rooms down on your right," Betty offered.

As the confused fellow gathered up his things and scurried out, Jack and Betty introduced themselves and invited everyone else to say their names in turn. The class was run more like a relaxed Amway meeting than a meditation class. The Astral Score subsided while a few people took turns testifying about interesting and even weird things that had happened to them since the last class. One had been offered a new business opportunity, exactly as she had visualized in an exercise. Another was having very intense and richly detailed dreams about avocados and pico de gallo salsa that seemed powerfully significant in some way that he could not yet figure out. He wondered if it had anything to do with a breathing exercise they had practiced.

Jack shrugged and Betty just said, "Could be."

Another class member said she kept catching glimpses out of the corner of her eye of an old man, very bent, walking with a stick. When she would look up at the old man, though, she would find nothing there. It sounded like someone was playing an ancient and rusty Theremin, somewhere off in the distance.

"This first level of exercises," Jack explained, "is called the Atem level and the aim is ultimately to help you become aware of entities of every kind. There are entities everywhere and it takes a slight shift in the way we normally experience things to be able to perceive them as such. Over the last few years, some of our students have reported similar experiences – glimpses of human figures, visions or voices of departed relatives, the sensation of being touched by a hand or another body part, a feeling that someone was present, even if no one can be seen, and so on. We had one guy last year who saw cartoon monkeys with rainbow colored fur. The weird thing was, the monkeys gave him very accurate information about traffic conditions, search engine optimization, and lottery numbers," Jack said.

The Theremin came a little closer, soaring up and down like a glider in windstorm.

"Perhaps next time you see the old man," Betty added, "you can communicate with him. Find out who he is, what he wants."

"Why is it called the Atem level?" Joe asked.

"Atem is the German word for *breath*," Jack offered. "And we use breath in these exercises to express attention, among other things. Also Atem is *meta* spelled backwards, as in metaphysics or metaphor. It's a name we apply to one of our entities, a useful fiction of sorts, a god who helps us to learn about entities and the human mind. Atem opens the way between our world and the world of entities."

"Will he be joining us today?" Joe asked.

"Sure," said Jack. "He's always with us when we do these exercises."

"I can feel his presence right now," Betty added, smiling sweetly.

The Theremin screeched to a halt.

"No," said Joe, "I meant, here, now, like standing up there with you and teaching the class."

"Heh, heh," Jack shook his head. "When we talk about entities, it's a concept we use to describe a natural neurological process. Our minds have a kind of built-in pattern recognition ability – we notice when any part of our experiences seems to reflect a greater whole, what is sometimes called a *holon*. For instance, a corporation can be considered as a world unto itself, a smaller reflection of the world at large, though since it is smaller it may be biased in one direction or another. Or, in some religions, humans are held to be a reflection of the greater conscious called god. Now finding such patterns may be more a matter of where and how we look and we may actively create them by perceiving selectively. Such patterns of perception and information seem, thanks to that built in pattern-recognition thing, to display a kind of intelligence – so we refer to that construct as an entity. Atem himself is one of these entities, really just a useful idea, a metaphor for a dynamic system of information, a way of using our brains that allows us to get certain tasks accomplished. Sometimes people have visions of Atem, but we don't take this stuff too literally – he's not physically present like you and me. Does that make sense?"

"Less and less all the time," Joe said.

"Great!" enthused Betty. "What do you say we get into some practice?"

General agreement from all parts of the room.

"We're going to begin with some breathing exercises." Betty sounded as if she had repeated this information many times. "Breath is energizing to body and mind, very directly. There's nothing mystical about it; the body relies on the presence of oxygen to function and responds physiologically in different ways to different amounts of gases in the system. As well, it is a direct link to the unconscious mind. Breathing is a behavior that is usually outside of awareness and when we do turn our attention to breathing, it quickly falls under conscious control.

"Sit in a comfortable position with your spine upright." Betty and Jack sat on their sofa and waited a moment for seat shifting to settle down. The Middle Eastern melody played softly, with only a hint of percussion. "Now imagine a circle around you, with a diameter just slightly greater than your outstretched arms, with you in the exact center."

Joe imagined a black circle drawn on the floor around him, passing beneath the sofa on either side. The circle wavered unsteadily. One side would start to fade and Joe would put his attention there and another portion of the circle would evaporate. Before he could get too frustrated with the process, Betty continued:

"Inhale, filling your lungs completely, from bottom to top. As you inhale, allow your attention to expand to fill the circle. If it helps to imagine your aura as a particular color or glow that fills the circle, then add in that visualization."

Sounds of deep breathing issued from around the room. Somebody's nose whistled. Joe imagined his attention as a bright blue sphere, expanding to the limits of the circle as he filled his lungs.

"Exhale completely," Betty instructed. "As you exhale, draw your attention in to a tiny spot within the center of your chest."

The sigh of air escaping from thirty lungs filled the room, accompanied by a whistly nostril or two. Joe's blue sphere shrank smoothly into his chest.

"Continue to practice like this," Betty said, "filling the circle with every inhalation, contracting down to a single point in the center of your chest with every exhalation."

Joe expanded and contracted. With each breath, the blue sphere seemed to get a little brighter and a little denser. By the time Betty signaled for them to stop, Joe was feeling rather brighter himself, lit up like the first harbinger of an acid trip.

"The second part of this," Betty explained, "is exactly like the first part, except that when you inhale, expand your attention to fill the entire room. Ready? Take notice of the boundaries of the room. Now fill your lungs and allow your attention, your aura, to fill the room. Then, when you exhale, contract it down to a single point in the center of your chest."

On the first inhalation, Joe had trouble filling the room with his blue sphere, but by the second attempt, his aura met the walls and filled in the corners. After a few minutes of this, the effect was much more pronounced. The blue had become much denser, much brighter – glowing like a special effect at a rock show – and Joe was feeling extremely energized. The Astral Score increased in volume and the drum track built slightly in intensity.

"Okay," Betty started up again, "we can take this one step further. On your inhalation, expand your attention, your aura, to fill the largest area you can conceive: The city, the county, the state – maybe the world, the solar system, or the universe. As large as you can manage. And, again, when you exhale, contract your attention down to a single point in the center of your chest."

Joe's first inhalation gave his attention an expanse of at least a few miles. On the second inhalation he was straining to imagine the State of New York. But then his sense of scale seemed to shift and he found it very easy to imagine his attention expanding to include stars and planets and vast expanses of space. It wasn't the entire universe, perhaps, but it was a major chunk of celestial real estate. It was a very odd sensation, accompanied astrally by a furious techno dervish dance. And when he shrank it down into his chest, there was a palpable throbbing, like his body was hooked up to a massive engine of some kind, his legs vibrating in polyrhythmic counterpoint to his chest. He wondered if having so many stars and planets, so much interstellar dust and gas, inside him could cause indigestion.

Betty instructed the class to allow their breathing to return to normal and to bring their attention fully back into the room. The astral drum track played a final flourish and stilled. Joe opened his eyes and the room definitely looked a lot brighter. Other class members were also looking around and met Joe's gaze with a smile. One guy was cleaning out his nose with a kleenex. Marlena, a little spaced-out and flushed, had her attention tuned to Betty and Jack.

"Okay," Betty asked, "so what happened?"

Several class members volunteered descriptions of their experiences. One had a bright green sphere of attention that managed to get as large as the solar system. Another one couldn't see what her aura looked like at all, but could still feel it filling the whole galaxy and then condensing stars and nebulae into the center of her chest. A fat man sitting toward the back of the room reported that whenever he tried to get his attention beyond the room, he got confused and had to stop.

"Excellent responses all around," Betty commented.

The fat man looked confused. "I just felt like I should have been able to do more..."

"Everyone perceives these things in their own unique way," Betty explained. "There's no right response. The point is simply to be aware of what happens for you. With practice, you'll find that you can do more and different things with these exercises."

"You want some more? Ready for anotha exercise?" Jack leaned forward in his seat and began to lead them through the next exercise. "We'll start with a few more expansion and contraction breaths. For this exercise, pick an intermediate size to expand in. Think in terms of geography if you can: the neighborhood, the city, the river valley, or whatever the right size seems for you. It's less important to know all tha details about Poughkeepsie than to just have a good idea what size your slice of real estate or reality's gonna be."

He paused for a minute or two while deep breathing played rhythm section to a nostril solo and the Astral Score oozed melodic ambience.

"Listen attentively to everything around you," Jack continued, his tone lowering slightly and his Garden State bark softening. "Listen in three dimensions, so that you become aware of sounds that are in different locations around you, above you or below you. Listen to the sounds that are close and the sounds that form the auditory background – wind, birds, distant cars, trains, boats, or whatever there might be."

In the room itself Joe heard a faint shifting of clothing, breathing, and allergy symptoms. He couldn't hear any wind or birds, but there was an increasing rumble that could only be the Amtrak train.

"As you continue to listen, look at everything that is within your sight. Notice color, movement or stillness, brightness, contrast, and so on. Notice what is close and what is farther away. Visualize what cannot be immediately seen – whatever is behind you, whatever might be associated with the more distant sounds that you hear, whatever you might already know about the surrounding location."

Joe's attention played around the room: Marlena sitting cross-legged on her rug, other students in various states of sitting and repose, the guy with the tissue up his nose again, Betty and Jack observing the group, smiling. He was aware of the shapes and sizes of the sofas and chairs behind him, the heads and shoulders of people emerging from them. He knew the colors of the rugs, the texture of the walls, the parts of the room hidden in shadow and the parts that glowed in light. And somewhere to the north, he could make out the speeding bullet shape of the approaching locomotive. It was all memory and imagination, Joe thought, encouraged by Jack's hypnotic delivery. And yet whenever he turned his attention to something in particular, the fabric of a sofa, someone's face, the side of an Amtrak car, he saw it in full color and with remarkable detail. He could make out the number 69 and the word "Acela" on the nose of the train – and he had no idea if Amtrak trains said any such thing.

"As you continue to listen and to look, extend your sense of feeling to whatever is immediately in your presence. How does it feel to sit where you are sitting? How do your clothes feel? How does the air feel on any exposed skin? Then imagine the feeling of those things that you can hear, see, or visualize. Will the floor feel smooth, rough, hard, soft, wet, dry, or whatever? How does the distant wind feel on skin? What does the upholstery in one of those distant cars feel like? And so on, with a large number of kinesthetic details about what is not immediately in contact, but can be heard or seen.
Stay and experience in this way, with all senses involved, for a few minutes."

Again Jack fell silent for a few minutes, watching the faces of his hypnotic subjects intently. Joe's mind wandered around, feeling things. The slightly fuzzy surface of the sofa next to him, the smoothness of the floor, the woolliness of the rug, the softness of Marlena's butt – by force of will, he pulled his attention from that soft spot and soared out into the parking lot, where he could feel the hard metal and plastic of various vehicles – and then the roar of the Amtrak suddenly surged to its peak and Joe's mind was aboard the train, sitting in a wide, reclining seat. A middle-aged woman in a flowered blouse sat across the isle, a small boy of about seven or eight napping in the crook of her arm. A discarded newspaper lay on the seat next to Joe, folded open to reveal an article entitled "What will you do on QYFJ Day?" That old Theremin wailed like a train whistle and then the noise of the train was fading to the south and Jack was saying, "Okay, come on back here. Come on back!"

It took a moment to reorient to the room and Joe could see others experiencing the same process. Some were turning around in their seats to see what was *really* behind them. Others discreetly stroked the upholstery to test the accuracy of their imagined feelings.

As the astral ambience melted away, Jack led a short discussion of the exercise. Almost everyone reported odd or surprising perceptions of things behind them or out of the room. Several people, like Joe, described taking short train rides.

"Good stuff," Jack said. "Remember what you experienced. When you go outside later, you can confirm more details."

Jack nodded at Betty and she stood. "This next one is a standing up exercise. Everybody up!" She waited as class members got to their feet.

"Start by thinking about a particularly pleasant and powerful experience that you've had, something with a good feeling that you'd like to experience again." She paused for a moment. "Does everyone have an experience you'd like to work with?"

Joe had several seconds of internal struggle. His experiences of late had not been particularly pleasant, even after his neurological revisions. The only recent thoughts that brought good feelings involved fleeting moments with Esty, but he was hesitant to use those. They seemed sacred to him in some way and, unsure of where this exercise was leading, he didn't want to mess with them. He sorted through a great variety of life events, most of them either inconsequential or somewhat depressing. Even his moments of supposed on-air triumph always seemed tinged by anxiety and self-doubt. But he did come to one that seemed pure and unadulterated. Well, pure enough at any rate. It was the day that Jerry Hull e-mailed him to say they were going to go with his show proposal. It ended several weeks of nervousness, alcohol, and self-castigation. The feeling was... elation. Relief. And most importantly – a moment of self-worth. A moment in which he knew that someone, somewhere actually liked him, had recognized that he was good for something.

"Okay," Betty continued, her voice shifting into a hypnotic rhythm and the Middle Eastern techno kicked in. "Remember what you saw when you were having the experience. Notice any motion or stillness in your field of vision. Notice the quality of the light and the quality of the colors. Notice if the things you see are near or far away." She paused.

Joe's memory filled in details: the computer screen, the e-mail window with Jerry's return address at the top, and the terse message in a typewriter-like font: Everyone likes your proposal. We're picking up your show. I'm sending contracts by snail mail. Jerry.

"Remember what you heard when you were having the experience. Notice any sounds or silence. Notice if the sounds are loud or quiet, if they are tones, rhythms or voices. Notice any background sounds in the environment of your memory."

And auditory details filled in: his own excited breathing, maybe even the beating of his heart. His own voice saying, "About fucking time!" and maybe even "Woohoo!" The sounds of traffic and people outside. The hum of the computer.

"Remember what you felt at the time. Remember what position your body was in, if you were moving or still. Remember the temperature of the air on your skin."

Joe recalled the way the chair felt beneath him. The way his hand felt on the computer's mouse. The dampness of his sweaty shirt. The warmth of the air.

"As you continue to recall more and details of the experience," Betty instructed, "notice where in your body the pleasant feeling begins and where it moves to as the experience develops. Notice what kind of a feeling it is, if it is temperature, tingling, pressure, movement, texture or however you might experience it."

It was a feeling of lightness in his chest, as if the weight that had constricted his breath for eons was finally released. A feeling of expansiveness that started in his lungs and spread upward and downward to his head and his abdomen. It was sort of like opening a bedroom window to a cool spring breeze and wafting away the rancid funk of winter's sour laundry.

"Give the feeling a color or colors. If this feeling had a color, what would it be? Apply that color or colors everywhere in your body that you identify the feeling.
Notice the shape and movement of the color in your body. For a state to maintain over time, it needs to cycle or pulse. If yours is cycling or pulsing, then accentuate that cycle or pulse, make it move faster or bigger or whatever enhances your experience. If your experience is not already cycling or pulsing, then imagine that it is… loop it back around so that it forms a cycle, then accentuate that cycle. This is called an Energy Flow."

Joe's feeling glowed a bright, light green, like neon light shining through a mist. It pulsed slightly in synch with the Astral Score. He took a deep breath and encouraged it to pulse more, filling his entire body with lightness and color.

"Accentuate it even more," Jack suggested. "Fill your entire body with the color, from head to toes. Make the colors richer, more vibrant. Add sparkles, shimmers, or glows if they increase the intensity of the experience."

The green color got brighter, more luminous and shimmered around the edges. As Joe imagined this, the feeling become even more intense, more pleasurable. He sighed and noticed that his face felt funny.

"Okay," Jack continued. "Enjoy that feeling for a moment and then just let it well up in you and express it as a gesture or simple movement. If the feeling were a gesture, what would it be?"

Joe found himself raising his arms over his head, turning around and then letting his arms float down to his sides again. It felt good. He did it again and heard astral French horns.

"That's right," Jack said. "Repeat it a few times so that you commit it to memory." He waited as the class followed his instructions and then asked, "Ready for tha fun part? Pick a partner to work with."

Marlena was looking at him and Joe joined her on the red rug.

"Stand facing each other," Jack instructed, "and teach each other your movement. Keep the original experience that you had, that you used to develop the movement – keep that to yourself, just demonstrate your movement."

Marlena's gesture was a gentle swaying of the body while her hands made a wavelike movement in front of her. Astral sax moaned soulfully. Joe caught on in a few repetitions and Marlena likewise quickly picked up on Joe's.

"Okay," said Jack. "Make your own gesture and watch your partner make his or hers. As you watch, start to combine your gestures. Between tha two of you, create a gesture that is a compromise or combination of tha gestures. Do it silently, please."

This proved slightly more challenging than it sounded. Joe found it puzzling, at first, to pay attention to the way Marlena was moving while his own body was doing something different. It was the cognitive equivalent of rubbing your belly while patting your head. Discordant horns tried to find "one." He glanced around the room and saw others apparently having the same challenge. One young guy was trying to teach what looked like a tai chi move to an older woman. Another pair, closer to Joe, looked like wallflowers at a high school dance, forced to be funky and giggling at their own ineptitude. Some of the more experienced class members, though, were already creating a combined gesture. Joe turned his attention back to Marlena.

Marlena had already incorporated Joe's turning around move into her movement. Joe noted that her hand movements started just as she came back around and he added that to his own gesture. It felt good. In another few moments, they had completely synchronized. Sway, turn around, wave your arms. It felt really good and the horn section found a funky groove. It was sexy. It was like being on stage with James Brown. It was like a great first kiss, awkward until it actually gets started, then a perfect sympathy of movement. Sway, turn around, wave your arms.

"That's just great," Jack exulted after a few minutes. "These are some great gestures. Okay, just stop right where you are. Hold still in whatever position you find yourself in. Take notice of how you feel right now. The same as before? Different? Notice where in your body you have this feeling and what kind of a feeling it is. If the feeling had a color, what would it be? Apply that color everywhere in your body that you have the feeling. Notice where it is and what it does. Does it cycle or pulse? Accentuate it. Have it move through more and more of your body. Make the colors richer and more vibrant. Add some special effects, sparkles, shimmers."

Joe's original neon green had somehow shifted to bright purple and it cycled through his entire body, from his toes up to the top of his head. The feeling was like warm purple starlight infused with champagne bubbles. His French horns melded with the techno undercurrents.

"Look at your partner. Now, use your hands to show your partner which way your feeling cycles or pulses in your body."

Joe showed Marlena how his feeling ran up his front and down his back. She was making almost the same gesture – her feeling also came up the front of her body and down the back. Joe's face felt even funnier and he realized that he was grinning from ear to ear.

"Now connect your feelings, your colored flow of energy, with your partner's colored flow. Where yours goes down, let it flow into your partner where his or her's goes up. Maybe it's a big circle, maybe it's a figure eight, maybe it's something else, but let your colors merge into one big cycle. Get closer to each other, if you want. You can touch if it's acceptable to both of you."

Marlena stepped up to Joe and squashed her buxom front against him. The energy flow took care of itself. With almost no effort, Joe was aware of a single cycle of colored imagination running between and through them, a big loopy figure of shimmering purple light that went down his back, up her front, down her back, and then up his front. The Astral Score became tasty acid jazz.

And the feeling intensified by an order of magnitude. They both sighed simultaneously and then gasped. It was like having your insides tickled with a feather duster while friendly warm hands stroked your skin. It was like bathing in mint sauce while drinking hot toddies. It was like the static electricity from a thousand long-haired cats rubbing your legs, thighs, butt and everywhere else. And something odd happened. Faint tendrils of purple light began to appear between them. Not imagination, not visualization as the rest of this all seemed to be. But light. Real, visible, glowing light. Joe looked at the other partner-groups scattered around the room. Many of them looked wonderfully blissful, as if their genitalia were conjoined rather than their imagination. But there were no visible flashes of light anywhere else, except around Joe and Marlena. It was similar to what had happened when he kissed Esty in his apartment, but not quite. No one else seemed to notice and Marlena had her eyes closed now.

After a few minutes, Jack called them back. There were scattered giggles, sighs, a woohoo or two, and one "Do we have to?" Chuckles from Betty and Jack.

"Whoa," Marlena said quietly to Joe, "That was sure something!" She joined him on the couch. He now felt oddly comfortable and natural sitting next to her. He had the urge to put his arm around her, but refrained. The Astral Score faded considerably, but never quite disappeared.

Jack elicited some discussion. Everyone seemed to have powerful experiences – yet no one described the open-eye visuals, the traces of purple light, that Joe had seen. He kept it to himself, and if Marlena had also seen them, she also stayed silent on the subject.

"Okay," said Jack. "Some of you may already be thinking about the possibilities of this one."

Marlena looked at Joe and arched an eyebrow.

"It's essentially the same as some forms of tantric yoga practice," Betty explained. Some of the class members looked knowing, others had blank stares. There was a bit of tittering from the back of the room. "Yes," Betty continued, "that means sex. Because some of you may wish to explore this on a more personal level, we're going to break here and let you take your practice off to a more private place, if you wish.

Remember, it's about the energy flow, not necessarily about the sex, though you'll find some surprising things if you experiment in that way. Some of you are here with partners that you arrived with and some of you have just met for the first time. Do only as much as is acceptable and appropriate for you! If your partner wants to keep this non-sexual, then by all means, keep your pants on!"

A man sitting off to the left of Joe raised his hand. "Um, exactly... uh, how...?"

"For first time exploration with this exercise," Jack explained, "we recommend a face-to-face seated position. Traditionally, this is called *yabyum posture*. Betty?"

Betty smiled and the two instructors slid off the couch and onto the rug. Jack sat crosslegged and Betty eased herself gently onto his lap, facing him, and wrapped her arms and legs around him.

"It's more fun with your clothes off," Jack grinned, "but you get the idea. Go really slow. In fact, remain still if you can. Then create your energy flows and hook them up."

Betty gave Jack a quick kiss on the lips and then they disentangled themselves and stood.

"Some of you have rooms here in the building and some are just visiting. You can use your rooms, of course, or you are welcome to use one of the lounge areas to practice in," Betty said, adding moderately confusing directions to the lounge areas.

"Okay," Jack commanded, "go to it!"

The Great Purple Hoo-Ha

27 ✶ **Research**

As they filed out into the bustling hallway, Marlena hooked an arm around Joe's waist and bumped her curvaceous hip against him. "Oh, baby," she said. "I been waiting for this!"

"Me too." Joe pulled out his palmcorder and held it up.

"You're going to tape us, too?" She feigned heat stroke, waving her hand in front of her face.

"Not us," said Joe. "*Them*." He hooked a thumb toward the class members emerging from the doorway behind them. "This is a perfect opportunity to do a little research. Let's get some of this on tape. Then we're going to go find Wilderman."

"Do I get a rain check?"

"Yeah, sure, what the fuck," Joe agreed, fiddling with the controls on the camera.

"You're just too sweet," Marlena said sincerely. "I am going to hold you to that, too. Mm, hmm."

He led the way, following what he could remember of Betty's directions, through a maze of halls and doorways. They followed the flow of foot traffic around a corner. A girl and a boy on hi-tech skateboards dodged around them and then they were engulfed by a pack of bearded men in flowing robes. Between the robes and whiskers, Joe caught a glimpse of a familiar face from the class and, grabbing Marlena's arm, pulled her free of the fuzzy newagers and they followed their classmate down a narrow side hallway.

A door at the end of the hall accepted Joe's keycard, winked a little green light and clicked open to reveal the lounge. Joe's idea of a lounge involved vinyl-upholstered booths and plenty of booze. Marlena's conception had something to do with either reclining lawn furniture or live piano music. This lounge, however, was a big warehouse room with a high ceiling, decorated to resemble a park. A wide path meandered through big potted trees and shrubs. The plants grew green and lustrous in pools of bright artificial light. Dimmer, shady areas offered patches of thick green carpet in lieu of lawn. There were a few park benches as well as softer sofas, hammocks, futons and piles of cushions. Bright, tinkling music issued from hidden speakers and merged eerily with a hint of astral Theremin.

Hoo-Ha adherents were scattered in pairs (and at least one threesome) throughout the soft and shady places (and in one case, in the middle of the path). Some were dressed and meditating or practicing breathing exercises. More were in various stages of disrobement and exploring not only the yabyum posture that Jack and Betty had demonstrated, but other positions as well, some requiring such flexibility and dexterity that it gave Joe a moment of awe. The awe was well-mixed with confusion and a fair twinge of arousal. But Joe's mission overrode his other feelings. He raised the video camera to his eye and began to creep among the foliage, framing choice erotic scenarios. Marlena stretched out on a park bench and watched with relaxed, professional curiosity.

Joe's efforts at stealth were perhaps wasted. It was difficult to hide completely in the big, open room. When practitioners did notice him, however, they simply smiled. Or even waved cheerily. He was, after all, Joe.

In a bower of vines that climbed up an arc of wires, a young couple copulated slowly in yabyum, the girl softly reciting instructions to the boy. Nearby, only somewhat hidden by a row of small potted trees, a grossly obese, middle-aged couple grunted and groaned as if they were shoveling bricks rather than seeking mystical union. Joe captured fabulous footage of two long-bearded men, their bodies entwined together within a single robe. He crept around a giant dieffenbachia and recorded the efforts of a beautiful blonde woman and a magnificently endowed dark-haired man, as they apparently came to fruition. They both cried out something that sounded like "ARRR-ROO-ARRRR," then fell exhausted onto the faux lawn. Off to one side, a black man with long dreadlocks was twisted like a pretzel with a red-haired older white woman. These two were almost entirely still, breathing in perfect synchronization. Through his viewfinder, Joe swore that for a moment he saw a hint of orange, crackly lightning around them. When he looked up from the camera, if there had been any remarkable effects, they were gone.

At the base of a very large banana tree, Joe immortalized several minutes of a threesome – all women – whose naked legs twisted together into a complicated knot. When he had enough footage, he stood up straight and turned to find someone standing right behind him.

"You son of a bitch," Petey said. His right hand aimed a device that looked like a small taser.

Joe stuffed his palmcorder back into a pocket – and ran. Behind him there was a snap as the taser electrocuted a glossy Hawaiian woodrose shrub. Joe dodged around trees and flowerpots, benches and lounge chairs, and the room's groaning and murmuring occupants. Petey charged after him. Both were inept runners and the chase happened in frustratingly slow motion. Finally, with Petey still twenty feet behind him, coming around a grove of Fichus, Joe found a door set in an alcove along one wall. He quickly dipped his keycard and slipped through.

He found himself in a wide hallway. Just ahead, an intersection of halls offered four choices of direction. Joe turned left and kept running. The people down this hallway looked like computer programmers on Casual Friday. They stopped to smile and wave as Joe ran by. He thought he caught a glimpse of Petey behind him, so he pulled open the nearest door, ducked inside and closed the door firmly behind him.

As the Astral Score played an ethereal arpeggio, Joe turned to face what looked like the front yard of a schizophrenic neighbor during holiday season. The room was full of lighted plastic lawn figures, dazzling in multicolored light. But it wasn't just Santa and a manger scene. It was a mass-produced, extruded plastic gathering of every known pantheon, and a few more. Nearest to Joe were the Hindu gods: Shiva's dance, Kali's rattling skulls, Ganesha's endless snack, and Hanuman's monkey capers frozen in translucent colors. Beyond them he saw Odin, Thor, Frey and Loki, inner bulbs glowing brightly. Egyptian gods formed a great rank of animal-headed figurines as the denizens of Mount Olympus cast holiday cheer before them. Haitian Voodoo loas blinked on and off along one wall and on a higher shelf, illuminated heads of J. R. "Bob" Dobbs alternated with glowing figures of Elvis and Jim Morrison.

From out of the glaring plastic a less radiant figure emerged, a chubby old woman in a lab coat, jabbing at a handheld computer with a stylus. She looked up to see Joe, froze for a moment and then broke into a wide grin.

"You're… him!" she exclaimed. "I'm so glad you're here! Did the Founder send you?"

"Um... yeah, sure," Joe nodded. "Whatever you want to believe."

"Oh, this is so wonderful! This will help my work so much!"

"Uh, right." Joe was confused.

"Just hold on," the old woman said, setting her computer down between the horns of a glowing plastic Pan. "Let me get my camera!" She scurried off along a row of twinkling nymphs and dryads.

Fine, Joe thought. A fan. No problem. If he hid here and autographed photos for a few minutes, it would give Petey enough time to get lost.

She returned a moment later toting a very unusual camera. It was as big as her head, with three flaring lenses emerging from the front. The back was covered with blue, green and red indicator lights and a long cable trailed off behind it. She fitted the camera onto a stand that was mounted on a track set into the floor.

"Okay," the old woman smiled nervously, "please come stand over here, Joe." She motioned toward where she wanted Joe to be, an X marked in gaffer's tape on the floor. He took his place and she squatted behind the camera, fiddling with buttons and dials. The camera emitted a series of muted beeps.

"Just about ready," the woman said, eliciting a few more beeps from the controls. "Take the pose you want and then hold perfectly still until I say so. Ready?"

Joe struck his favorite pose, the one he used at the beginning of each show, a wide stance, skewed at an angle to the audience, gesturing welcome with one hand and looking up slightly. Suddenly the camera was clicking rapidly and humming as it slid along its track, making a rapid circle all the way around Joe. In a few seconds it returned to where it began, gave a final click and a beep and then stopped.

"Great! Great!" the old woman exulted. "Hold the pose! One more for safety!"

The camera hummed and clicked around him a second time and finally the woman gave him permission to relax. "All done! Thank you very much, Mr. Schmoe. This really means a lot to us."

"Fuck you, old bitch," Joe snapped, then thought better of it and smiled. "But maybe you can help me now."

She nodded, oblivious to the insult, waiting expectantly.

"Do you know where I can find Wilderman?"

"The Founder is usually in the Level 10 zone," she said. "Do you know how to find it?"

Joe shook his head and the old woman gave him a set of complicated instructions. He thought he had the general gist of it, thanked her and backed cautiously out into the hall. There was no sign of Petey and Joe set off in the direction the woman had indicated.

He roamed down the hallway, made a series of turns, and passed through a big common area where the full eclectic range of Hoo-Ha weirdoes and nerds relaxed, chatted, and drank coffee from paper cups. Then he went up a narrow stairway, through a keycard-entry door, and into a hallway that looked like a cross between a hospital ward and the upper floor in a luxury hotel. Joe took out his camera and shot a few moments of video, but it was a pretty sedate scene, with neither nudity nor overt weirdness and he put the cam away again. The denizens of this level of Hoo-Ha H.Q. were generally well-dressed, or at least normally-dressed. Some had the look of doctors or maybe psychiatrists and an occasional techie in a lab coat pushed some piece of arcane equipment – things with meters and small computers wired in clusters – down the hall. A door opened and as a doctor emerged, Joe caught a glimpse of a young man lying on an examining table, writhing in either agony or delight – it was difficult to tell. The door clicked shut behind the doctor, who stopped to gawk at Joe through thick horn-rimmed glasses. The man wore an ID tag that read "Dr. Schwagbole."

"Hey," the doctor exclaimed, "aren't you...? You're...?"

"Yeah, yeah," Joe said. "It's me. What goes on here? What's this place for?"

"Oh, this is a little pet project of the Founder's," Dr. Schwagbole explained. "We're developing a cure for most kinds of what is usually called mental illness. Psychosis, depression, anxiety, obsessive-compulsive disorders, personality disorders. So far it's just a research project and a service we can offer to a few of our longer-term associates here."

"You can... cure mental illness?" Joe was skeptical. "Why don't more people know about this?"

"Someday they will," the doctor said. "Perhaps when the Hoo-Ha comes."

"Right. The Hoo-Ha," Joe nodded. "So tell me, where can I find the Founder this time of day?"

"He's usually working now, but I'm sure he'll find time to see you." Schwagbole offered some complicated directions to the Level 10 zone.

The door that the doctor had recently emerged from swung open and the young man that Joe had glimpsed stepped out.

"Thanks, doc!" the man enthused, clapping the doctor heartily on the back. "That was awesome! When's my next session?"

At that moment, another door down the hall burst open. Petey jumped into the hallway, adopted a martial crouch, and pointed the taser at Joe.

Joe turned and ran through a doorway, up another flight of stairs, then dodged through a series of sparsely populated hallways. He stopped to catch his breath in an alcove by an elevator. He could hear the elevator descending in its shaft. It had no buttons to press, only a keycard slot. Joe stuck his card in. It beeped and the light flashed red. He tried it again: beep, red light. But the elevator car approached.

Petey, Joe thought. He darted around a corner and flattened himself against a doorway. He could hear the elevator door open. Holding his breath, he peered around the corner. It wasn't Petey. It was two young women in skimpy silk robes. The elevator door stayed open, so he ran for it and jumped into the car. The women turned, saw it was him, smiled and giggled until the door slid shut.

Joe inspected the controls. The elevator apparently only made four stops, two below the floor he was on, and one above. The one above said *Level 10 Zone*. He pushed the button and began to rise.

28 ✶ Level 10 Zone

The elevator doors opened to reveal a lounge area of a different kind. It was a bit smaller and cozier, more like a posh hotel suite than a park. A few potted plants draped glossy leaves over thick carpets, overstuffed chairs and giant pillows. Joe stepped off the elevator. The doors closed behind him and the car immediately began to descend.

From somewhere that Joe couldn't see, a deep voice boomed. "Hello? Who's there? Girls, did you come back? We're a bit busy right now."

Joe pulled out his camera and silently stalked the voice. Or rather, voices. As he got closer, he could hear a soft female voice, murmuring, reciting something, oblivious to the booming of the other voice. There was music playing and at first Joe thought it was the Astral Score: bassy electronica, with some old school Theremin.

"Hello?" The voice called. "Who the hell is that?"

Joe crept around a big leather sofa, through the leaves of a giant potted fern, and in a moment he had the source of the voice in his viewfinder: a big man, really big, with short, dark, spiky hair and penetrating dark eyes. He was entirely naked, sitting crosslegged on a large pillow, facing Joe. On his lap, in yabyum position, her back to Joe, was a small, deliciously curvy, naked woman, still chanting or murmuring or whatever she was doing.

There was an astral guitar fanfare.

It had to be, Joe thought. He fit the description. A big man, doing his thing here in the most inner sanctum of the

Hoo-Ha headquarters. Wilderman. Practicing sex magick. He couldn't have asked for anything more. It was the perfect scene for Sex Lives of Cult Leaders. Astral Theremin howled along with the muzak. The camera hummed as it gathered footage.

"Oh," the man said, as his eyes pierced the dim light and rested on Joe. "It's you. I thought you'd be here much sooner, Joe."

The woman stopped chanting. "Joe?" she asked, turning her head to see.

Joe caught a glimpse of the woman's face and almost dropped the camera. Later, he was amazed that he kept shooting.

It was Esty.

Sort of.

It was Esty, but she looked different. Perhaps not quite older, but riper. Deeper curves in her waist and hips, a fuller, rounder face, fuller lips. But still Esty, impaled on the Founder's lap, her cheeks flushed with passion.

Behind him, Joe could hear the elevator climbing its shaft, returning.

"Esty?" he croaked as the camera continued to whir.

"Will… The Founder," she said, "is helping me out with my project…"

The camera kept rolling. "*He's* helping *you*?"

"That's right," Wilderman boomed. "You have no idea how important Esty's project is to us…" He began to lift Esty from his lap.

"Oh, sure," Joe said. "I'll have to remember that line. 'It's important that you fuck me because it will bring the end of the world.' Right."

"Joe," Esty said, "I'm confused. I thought you'd understand. You of all people..." She was starting to look a little more like the Esty he knew, curves smoothing out again to a nineteen-year-old body.

Joe scowled. The camera wavered.

"Really," she said, "I was the one who asked him. I'm onto something. A way to change, to become my perfect self."

"Goddamnit," Joe said. "Fuck!"

Back in the other part of the lounge, the elevator beeped softly and the door slid open. The Astral Score struck some ominous chords. Dum-dum-dummm!

Esty wrapped a robe around her lean body. Now she looked very familiar again, the slim and delicate girl he'd met a few days ago. She smiled. "I knew you'd understand! Thank you, Joe!"

Petey burst through the fern leaves, taser already aimed. Joe shut off the camera and turned to face him.

"You son of a bitch," Petey said. "How dare you spy on us? How dare you spy on our Founder in his most private place? Why I oughta..."

"Whoa! Petey!" Wilderman boomed. "Why are you treating our honored guest like this? This is Joe! *Joe*! Put that thing away."

Petey slowly and reluctantly lowered the taser partway. "Can't you see what he's doing? What he does to everyone? He's fooled you all. Even you, Bill."

"I'm pretty sure I know who and what Joe is," Wilderman said more softly. "Stand down, Petey. I have a story to tell that may help us all to understand this situation."

"A story. Fine," Joe said. "Any chance you could put some pants on first?"

The Great Purple Hoo-Ha

29 ✱ Fucking Tornadoes

Joe planted his ass in a big, soft chair and Esty sat in another, facing him. Petey claimed some floor that placed him between Joe and the elevator and he kept his hand nonchalantly near the taser.

Wilderman remained where he was seated, still no pants, but a blanket now pulled over his lap. He spoke softy, though his deep voice still filled the space while haunting Theremin and ringing, jangly guitar played either from a speaker hidden somewhere or from the Astral Score; Joe found it difficult to tell which.

"I don't know how familiar you are with this part of the world," Wilderman began. "When I first moved to this area, we didn't have tornadoes around here. You never heard about them. You never saw them. They were something that happened in trailer parks far away, or in the Kansas of someone's imagination."

Either Joe or Petey – or both – must have looked fidgety. "Now bear with me," Wilderman continued. "This definitely relates to the situation.

"When I was in my early twenties, I got involved in a local theater company. We were based in the little town of Saugerties, up the river a bit, to the north. Now you have to understand something about the arts scene up here. It's full of people who moved out of Manhattan and people who want to be like people from Manhattan. Especially in theater – New York City is where it's at. So as far as local theater goes, you can push the limits a bit more than in other small towns. That's not to say that you'll get an audience for your weird and experimental productions, just that no one will run you out of town for making them.

"So I was in a play. It was an existential, absurdist piece about men and women and how they always want to be free but somehow only end up pissing each other off. All the male characters in the play wanted to sleep with all the women and all the women wanted to create art that only occasionally involved the men or sex. This greatly confused the men, who thought that the women's sporadic interest meant that the women secretly, madly lusted for them all the time. And it greatly confused the women, who thought that the men's ongoing ardor meant that they, too, would sacrifice themselves for art. The only character that seemed to have a clue was a dog that indiscriminately humped the legs of men, women, chairs, tables, and any artwork he could reach.

"The dog was a casting problem. We needed a dog who could act and actors who could act while having their legs humped. We found a dog at the local pound, a little white and black mutt that was about the right size and excessively horny. We had no idea if the dog could act, but it was pretty much our only option. However, nobody involved in the play wanted to keep little Horndog in their own home and after one visit, the dog was banned from the rehearsal space as well. So we bribed a guy at the pound to keep the little nipper in lockup just a bit longer."

"Excuse me," Joe interrupted. "Tornadoes?"

"Right, right," Wilderman boomed jovially. "We're getting to the twisters. You see, it was opening night and there I was, heading across town with my co-star, the woman who also wrote and directed the piece, to pick up the dog and go to the theater. We were out walking in the late afternoon sun and she was having reservations about the whole thing. We had a horny dog who never rehearsed and, on top of that, she was worried that she hadn't worked on her lines enough and would forget them when the time came. I confessed that I, too, hadn't really put enough time into the project and probably didn't know my lines. However, since no one else had ever seen the play, I argued, it didn't really matter whether we got the lines right or not. As long as we sort of got the gist of the story, which was pretty conceptual and abstract to begin with, then no one but us would be the wiser.

"This calmed her a bit. In spite of not knowing how to act in a particular situation, she had at least a little bit of confidence in her own ability to think creatively and make the right choice in the moment. And then, when we were still half a mile from the pound, some damned ugly clouds started rolling in. They were dark, greenish black and they churned and pumped with energy. Ominous. The wind started blowing leaves and litter and crap all around us. And when we turned a corner and came out on top of a low hill with a clear view of the horizon, we could see the tornadoes.

"There was one big motherfucker of a tornado, perhaps a mile wide where it touched ground, big and dark and just roaring like the end of the world was coming fast. You could see weird lights in the whirlwind and all kinds of debris flying out of it – splinters of houses, jagged sheets of torn metal, dust, rocks, trees, you name it. To the left of that big mother and slightly in the lead was a smaller satellite twister, something that looked a lot more like what I thought of as a tornado. It was a dark, spinning rope of wind that tossed up clouds of earth. The two of them were a few miles away, perhaps wreaking destruction on Kingston or West Hurley, and moving inexorably in our direction.

"We made it to the pound and picked up the dog. It required a bit of haggling and yet another bribe, so we were running a little late. We had to hustle to get back across town to the community hall that served as a local theater. When we got outside, though, the roar of the wind sounded like every freight train in the east was rolling our way at full speed. The twisters were close, really close, and shit was flying everywhere. The dust in the air felt like needles. But the show must go on and we pulled our jackets up over our heads and kept going.

"We almost made it, too, but then little Horndog wiggled free and started to run. I wanted to run the hell away from the tornadoes, but the damn dog had a hardon for the storms. Literally. He had already tried to hump everything else he encountered. Now it seemed he wanted to hump the writhing leg of the satellite tornado. He ran toward it, leaped up in the air and disappeared. We never saw the little guy again. And those damn twisters kept coming closer and closer. It looked like it was going to be the end."

Wilderman fell silent.

Petey snorted derisively. "Come on, Will. There's never been a tornado that big in New York State. It's just another one of your stories."

Wilderman was getting to his feet, the blanket wrapped around him like a toga. "Not *just* another story, Petey," he said. "Actually it was a dream I had the other night."

"A dream," Petey echoed. "So what are we supposed to learn from that?"

Long strides took Wilderman halfway to the elevator before he turned and said, "Simple. I woke up before the end of the world. Which is a strategy that I highly recommend. It beats fucking tornadoes."

Joe shook his head. "I'm not sure…"

The elevator door opened at Wilderman's touch and he stepped in. He turned and gave the others a cheery smile, the doors slid closed and Wilderman was gone.

The canned music in the lounge – and the Astral Score – ended with a flourish and fanfare of screaming guitar. Then there was silence.

Joe started to get to his feet and Petey jumped up to beat him to the high ground. "Look, Petey," Joe said. "I didn't mean to insult you earlier. I do it with everybody and most people are oblivious. It's just a game that keeps me amused."

"It's true," Esty vouched. "You should have seen him with the cab driver. I couldn't do it. It's a skill."

Petey stepped closer to Joe – a little too close – and stretched his gangly neck forward until their faces were inches apart. "Fuck you, Joe. You may be able to put one over on Wilderman, but not on me, asshole. I know what you're about. If you endanger any project on these premises, if you stand in the way of the Great Purple Hoo-Ha, I will take you down."

"Believe me," Joe said. "I couldn't care less about the Great Non-Existent Whatever. I'm just doing my job."

"And I'm just doing mine." Petey turned and walked to the elevator. He pushed the button, but the doors didn't slide open as they did for Wilderman. Somewhere, way down below, some machinery turned over. He pushed the button again and then had to wait, shifting his weight from one leg to the other, until the car finally arrived and the door opened. Joe and Esty looked at each other and remained silent.

Once Petey was gone, Esty came to Joe. "Joe, I'm so glad you understand. If it were anyone else, who knows what they might have thought, walking in on me, on Wilderman and me, like that. I know that what we do here is well outside the usual culturally-mandated belief system. Do you trust me that this is important? Really important?"

Joe had trouble forcing the words out. "I... have to leave now. Good bye."

He made for the elevator. "I'm so glad you trust me, Joe," Esty said. "Because I trust you."

30 ✶ Acid Cream

Joe's suit was impeccable and his hair was perfectly glued down. The audience was pumped, over the top with enthusiasm, screaming and hooting for him. But he wasn't feeling it. He knew the applause wasn't really for him. He knew they were applauding for the distorted mirror of their own perceptions. And he knew what a shit he really was. His theme music faded out and the Astral Score followed with a sad minor chord.

He read his cue cards listlessly. "Ladies and gentlemen – and the indeterminate creature in the second row there – welcome to another exciting episode of Joe's Show."

The audience screamed with glee.

"Over the past few weeks, we've explored some aspects of a new and emerging – we'll call it a cult for convenience, though it seems to be much more than that. This group predicts the coming of The Great Purple Hoo-Ha, a Rapture, a cataclysm, a transformation for the human race. While that's either a hopeful scenario or a very, very scary one, it seems to involve a lot of – yes, you guessed it – sex."

The audience hooted on cue.

"Last week we heard a little bit about the group's Founder, an elusive character named Wilderman. Now let me ask you – what do you think it's like to be the leader of a sex cult? That's right; tonight on Joe's Show we're offering you *The Sex Lives of Cult Leaders!*"

The audience went wild.

"Over the past week, I traveled to the city of Poughkeepsie, New York to personally investigate, to find out just what really happens in the giant Great Purple Hoo-Ha complex along the Hudson River. And I can tell you this: it's even wilder than you can imagine! Are you ready? We've got guests, we've got video footage, and we've got one hell of an exciting show," he said morosely.

Cheers. Even louder applause.

"Are you ready?" The cue card said *pause*, so Joe paused while the audience shouted their readiness.

"Let's get right to it, then," he said. "Roll the video."

The big monitors on either side of the stage lit up with a heavily-edited montage of Joe's palmcorder footage. Faces and private parts were blurred for on-air acceptability, but it was still great stuff. Couples coupling in yabyum posture. Groups linking limbs and moaning ecstatically. While the video sex played to hoots, cheers, and rapt, goggle-eyed attention, Joe walked onto the set and collapsed in his host chair. He contemplated his betrayal of people who trusted him and his exploitation of artificial charisma for ratings and money. It was fucked up.

The video ran for about three minutes, ending with a climax and a shout of ARRR-ROO-ARRRR! – and then the studio cameras zoomed in on Joe. He forced a smile, but it felt too awkward and he gave it up. The audience didn't care, they cheered even more.

"Our first guest you might remember from last week," Joe said. "Damon Dark, spokesman for The Great Purple Hoo-Ha. Welcome back, Damon."

"Thanks, Joe," Dark smiled with genuine charisma and warmth. He sat on Joe's sofa, his legs crossed.

"Can you explain a little bit about what we just saw?"

"I sure can," Dark uncrossed his legs and leaned forward. "This appears to be footage of students practicing various sex magick techniques. We offer the techniques in a safe and not-overtly-sexual classroom environment and then we turn the students loose to practice at their own pace and at the level of intimacy they are comfortable with. While the video we just saw focused on the more, hmm, erotic techniques, more typically you'd see a range of things happening, including students who choose to have no physical contact at all. You'll notice that there isn't too much movement in these techniques – the eroticism provides a sort of stimulus and a means of connection between people, but the real work is happening internally."

"Internally?" Joe asked, gesturing towards his innards. The audience thought it was hilarious.

"Oh, heh heh, well, that too," Dark chuckled amiably. "The work happens in our consciousness, our minds, our imagination – as well as in the nervous system, all the muscles, the skeleton. The genitals are just a tiny part."

"Not too tiny, I hope!" Joe read lamely from a hastily scrawled cue card. The audience was in stitches.

Damon leaned toward Joe. "Not in my case, at any rate." There were a few mild titters from the crowd.

"Okay," said Joe. "I've got to ask. How did all this come to be? How did Wilderman actually start teaching this stuff? Seems to me it would be quite a risk to get up in front of a group and say, 'All right, now everyone get naked and get it on!'"

Hoots. Guffaws.

Dark chuckled. "I don't know. This audience might be willing."

Applause.

"It *is* one of the more interesting stories about the Founder..." Dark waited for the astral fanfare. "...how he first started teaching his methods. When the Founder was young, one of his favorite authors, Bob Cunningham, taught a series of seminars at The School for New Learning, a famous newage center in northern California. Cunningham wrote books about what he called 'brain repatterning,' a process that seemed to involve a lot of breathing exercises and heavy-duty psychedelic drugs. The man was also famous for inserting electrodes into his own brain and wiring himself to the brain of a dolphin while dosed on a combination of LSD and cheap wine. The Founder thought that perhaps Cunningham had figured out some of the essentials of mind tech and he knew that he just had to attend the seminar. So he packed up a knapsack and a sleeping bag and rode a big, green hippie bus out to the west coast.

"The S.N.L. featured not only a beautiful outdoor seminar area, but also a natural cavern with hot springs where the newagers liked to soak their cosmic asses. Wilderman found the seminar to be absolutely fascinating. Cunningham showed up unbelievably stoned, mumbled incoherently about fruit-flavored aliens who kept their brains in oven mitts, and then fell out of his chair. Many of the attendees felt that their seminar dollars were going to waste, but the Founder realized that Cunningham was actually repatterning his brain right in front of them! He was giving them a live demonstration, rather than just talking about it, although Wilderman had to wonder if the new patterns that Cunningham etched on his gray matter were in any way useful.

"On the first evening of the seminar, the Founder wandered down to the hot springs and it blew his mind even more than the seminar. People were getting naked, seemingly without any embarrassment, and jumping right into the bubbling hot pool. There were more women than men and he was overcome with the wonderful diversity that he saw. There were skinny young women, large floppy-breasted women, athletic women with remarkable buttocks, and older women with flowing hair and wise eyes. The men were, for the most part, scholarly types with skinny limbs and pot bellies. Bob Cunningham floated at one end of the pool, masturbating gleefully and occasionally attempting to convince others of the imminent arrival of cream-filled pastry intelligence from another dimension.

"Wilderman peeled off his clothes and slid into the water. It was hot and good and he could feel his muscles start to soften now. While everyone pointedly refrained from staring at each other, the conversation inevitably found its way to the idea of brain repatterning.

"'I really wish Cunningham would just teach us the techniques,' one of the men complained. 'I mean, I'm not really sure what's he doing.'

"'Hydrogggg...' Cunningham commented from his end of the pool. 'Hydrogenated... hydrogen... ate... it...'

"Wilderman pointed out that Cunningham was doing it right here, repatterning his brain. 'It's historic,' the Founder said. 'You'll be able to tell your grandchildren that you saw Bob Cunningham fall out of his chair. How cool is that?'

"'I don't know,' a skinny young woman replied. 'I paid fifteen hundred bucks just to see this clown get wasted and play with himself. Hell, I could have stayed home and watched my family do the same thing!'

"'Creamy, creamy, creamy family,' Cunningham announced. 'Butter cream intelligence transcends belief.'

"'But brain repatterning is so damn intriguing,' Wilderman said. 'I mean, he's programming his beliefs to accept what we would normally think impossible or even absurd. Imagine if we could repattern all our brains to accept impossibilities like world peace, global consciousness or magical powers.'

"'Interdimensional structures of... of... hydrogenated flux cream,' Cunningham asserted. 'Trance fatty, acid.'

"'It sounds like you know something about it,' said an older woman with wise eyes.

"'Acid!' Cunningham screamed. 'Acid cream!'

"'I've practiced Cunningham's methods,' Wilderman admitted, 'ever since I first read the books.'

"They all looked at him with great respect. 'You read the books?' the older woman asked.

"'I tried to read them,' one of the men confessed, 'but it was beyond me. It seemed so obvious that there was something there... I came here hoping to understand.'

"'Flux!' Cunningham yelled. 'Flux you all!'

"'Show us,' said an athletic brunette. They all agreed that Wilderman had to show them.

"Now Cunningham's method of brain repatterning basically involved deep 'circular' breathing while zillions of acid molecules roamed through his brain. The Founder could show them the breathing technique, but he was all out of acid – and

Cunningham seemed to have eaten all of his – so he had to think of something else. When Wilderman was a teenager, he had a series of visions in which he was shown a set of spiritual techniques. He never shared the visions or the techniques with anyone... but now was his chance. So, sitting naked in the hot water, vapors of steam drifting around them in the cavern, Wilderman started teaching. First he showed them Cunningham's breathing method, which was simply to take very full breaths and entirely eliminate the pauses at the top and bottom of the breath so that it became a seamless and constant ebb and flow. When they were all breathing together, he started teaching them his own techniques to circulate energy through their bodies – and between them.

"To make a long story just a little bit longer," Dark continued, "the energy circulation that Wilderman taught them quickly became tangible to everyone. It flowed through them all in gorgeous colorful, humming waves. And drew them together. The closer they got to each other, the brighter and richer and more vibrant the energy waves became – until they were all in contact, so close that they were, well, inside of each other.

"At that moment, when they were all completely connected by the energy flow, there was an amazing flash of rainbow light that filled the cavern. The flash left a weird kind of after-image floating in the air which began to spin and suddenly flared out into a vast portal, opening on another dimension. Within the opening was indescribable fractal profusion, a vast complicated intricacy of shapes and details that defied comprehension.

"At the far end of the pool, Bob Cunningham began to rise out of the water, into the air, drifting gently, as if wafted by a breeze, toward the portal. 'Remember,' Cunningham said with sudden, surprising lucidity, 'every dream that you have is real, if you can only repattern your brain to conceive it that way. Transcend the boundaries of your beliefs!'

"They were all in total, deep communion, physically, mentally, and spiritually… and they were building toward a climax. They all knew what must happen when they came; it seemed inevitable. The intensity built and built and finally burst forth in a great brain-repatterning group moan, the newagers hanging onto each other tightly as they rode out the waves and spasms.

"'Éclairs!' Cunningham cried rapturously. 'Oh! Oh, my! Éclairs!'

"And Cunningham transcended the boundaries of everyone's belief by levitating into the portal, which imploded after him. There was another bright flash, a sonic shock wave that splashed water onto the walls of the cavern, and then it was gone, leaving only a group of naked and quite overwhelmed newagers soaking in a hot spring.

"That group stayed in touch with Wilderman and became his first ongoing students. Years later, they would teach the Founder's methods and recruit hundreds more aspirants to help bring humanity toward its inevitable goal, The Great Purple Hoo-Ha."

"Well, that was a remarkable story," Joe said with a total lack of enthusiasm. "What became of Cunningham? Did he come back from the portal?"

"Cunningham was never seen again," Dark said. "He was gone. The official story was that he got too stoned and drowned in the hot spring, but his body was never found."

31 ✶ Perpetrator

Damon Dark slid over on the couch to make room as Marlena strolled out onto the set. Her curves were packed tightly into an expensive evening gown loaned to her by the studio wardrobe department. Joe wondered about all the ways she could burst forth from her dress and figured the audience had similar thoughts. It was great for the ratings, but Joe didn't really care.

"Our next guest," he said weakly, "accompanied me on my fact-finding mission to Poughkeepsie. We lost track of each other during all the excitement, but I'm sure Marlena got a good eyeful of the action, too. Say hello to Marlena."

"Hello, everyone," she said, swinging her hindquarters onto the couch and crossing her legs. "I got much more than an eyeful. After you took off, Joe, I made some new friends. Mm, hm."

"I just bet you did," Joe read from the card, then waited as the audience went wild. When the hoots had died down a little, he said, "I'm sure what you did there is fascinating, Marlena, but I want to show the audience something else, something you told me on the ride up. Can we roll video, please?"

On the monitors, Joe's palmcorder footage, recorded in the limo, retold the story of Marlena and Billy the Weiner. The audience hooted and howled as Marlena posed for the camera and they listened in hushed amazement to the juicy bits of the tale. Joe slouched in his chair and rested his head in his hands. He was sliding in again, he knew it. Sliding back into the depths of his mind where his inner voice never ceased berating him. He considered that the voice probably went on and on all the time, it was just at these low moments that he tuned in. And the fucking voice was usually right, too.

Up on the monitors Marlena was saying, "You know, I think his last name actually might have been Wiener."

Closer to his core of being, Joe was telling himself how he was very likely fucking up a new – what? Religion? – a new *something* that it probably wasn't his business to fuck with. Maybe the Great Purple Hoo-Ha wasn't going to transform planet Earth as advertised, but it was no worse than a hundred other religions generally considered "good" by humans at large. And like those other forms of spirituality, the GPHH possibly had something to offer. A cure for mental illness? A brand new kind of sexual revolution? A new way of understanding the mind? Who knew? And he was fucking it all up. He was a traitor to humanity.

"I couldn't possibly imagine how something so enormous could possibly fit in my little tiny hole," video Marlena said. The audience howled with glee.

And then there was Petey. There were people out there who weren't fooled by Joe's false front, the mirror defense screen that Atem had created to hide his foulness. People out there who *knew*. Rex Massenclear. Atem himself. Maybe Wilderman; Joe wasn't sure. How many others? It didn't matter. That was enough. Petey. Yeah, Petey knew.

On the monitor, Marlena confessed, "I had the best view I'd ever had, in my fourteen years of life, of a massive wiener." Hoots. Cheers.

And he knew, too. He knew he was a faker, a poseur, a perpetrator, a fraud. He knew that everything that most – but not all! – of the people believed about him wass lies. Every good deed he was ever praised for was a sham, a hallucination, a shadow. Every kind word, every brilliant, creative choice, every funny line that he took credit for were only in the mind of the beholder. His paycheck, growing fatter each week, was unearned. The admiration of millions of fans was for a ghost, a phantom, not for him. And the adoration of the one person that he really adored – was based on the same lie.

"While I was getting up the nerve to reach over and touch it," the pre-recorded Marlena was saying, "there was a big, fat whoosh of a noise and a big, spinning whirlpool formed in front of us, out of thin air." The audience sat in hushed amazement.

Joe thought about Esty. He was confused and angry at her – and angry at himself for feeling that way. He had no right to be angry. If she really knew him, though, if she could see and hear and feel the real Joe – she would despise him. She hadn't lied to him, he had lied to her. Maybe he hadn't meant to, but, really, if she could see him as he really was – an opportunistic sleazebag capable of turning his beloved's highest aspiration into sleaze fodder, into titillation for the lowest common denominator.

"I got up and ran like hell!" Marlena recounted. "Which was probably the right thing to do, but I still got into all kinds of trouble."

And as angry as he was with himself, there was one other – person? – to be angry with. Atem. The goddamn Opener. That immaterial asshole who had cursed Joe in this way. Joe thought it would be his ticket to the good life – but it was a monkey's paw, it was Satan's trick violin, it was a Trojan whore, it was a sugar-coated turd.

"All they ever found was his clothes, out in the barn." Marlena's face was framed in close-up as the video came to an end.

"A remarkable story," Joe mumbled morosely.

"It was my pleasure," Marlena smiled.

"The reason we showed this now, the reason you're here now," Joe read from his cards, "is because we have a surprise for you."

"Ooh," Marlena cooed, "a surprise!"

"Our research department spent a little time with your story. We were hoping to find out what really became of Billy the Wiener. You know what we found out?"

"What? What did you find out?"

"We couldn't find any record of a Billy Wiener who disappeared from northern New Jersey around that time. But we did find someone else."

"Who? Who did you find?"

"There was no Billy Wiener. But there was a story that we found about a child who disappeared who fit the description you gave. That child's name was William." The cue card said *pause*, so he did. "William Wilderman. The man who began the Great Purple Hoo-Ha."

There was silence in the studio. The Astral Score played a pristine, clear-as-a-bell guitar fanfare.

"Billy the Wiener was Wilderman?" Marlena was wide-eyed. "Wilderman is Billy the Wiener?"

"That's right," Joe said. "He turned up again a few years later in upstate New York."

"Oh my god," said Marlena. "Oh my freakin' god."

"This is incredible," enthused Damon Dark. "Thank you Joe! Thank you Marlena! You've given us a new chapter in our records of the origin of the GPHH. And it speaks to the inevitability of it all. The synchronicity of it. That you, Marlena, would meet Wilderman again after all these years, it's just… just…"

"Improbable?" Joe suggested.

"Mm, hmm," Marlena averred.

"Fate," Dark said. "Destiny."

"Ah, who fucking cares?" Joe groaned. "It's all a lot of crap."

The audience whooped and cheered.

The Great Purple Hoo-Ha

32 ✶ Climax

"We've got one more thing to show you today," Joe told the audience.

The cue card read, *You want to see the The Sex Lives of Cult Leaders?*

Joe said, "I can't fucking believe I'm going to do this."

The words he was supposed to read were, *You want to see Wilderman? We've got Wilderman.*

Joe stared blankly at the camera for a long moment. He considered walking off the set right then and there. He considered apologizing publicly. He thought of the consequences of what he was about to do. What fucking consequences? They would love him anyway. *Esty* would love him anyway. Even if he was a traitor, a liar, and a damned idiot. That thought just made him feel even worse.

The audience waited with growing anticipation and excitement. What he finally said was, "Show the video. Show the fucking video of Wilderman screwing Esty. Go on! Show it!"

The astral fanfare was a grand one.

And there on the giant monitors, much, much larger than life, appeared the image of Wilderman, big, imposing, spiky-haired, rocking Esty on his lap. Even though she was only visible from the back and the lower part of the picture was blurred for television, her delicious curves were stunning. Seen at this screen-filling size, it was an incredibly erotic image. And it was Esty who drew the eye, Esty who, even though dwarfed by Wilderman, captured the imagination. Her shape was the very archetype of the feminine, her movements the primordial dance of creation. Joe's heart ached, twisted, crumpled, and tried to climb down into his intestines.

At first the audience was silent, awed. Then they exploded into hoots, cheers, whistles and wild applause. It was the climax to the show.

But not for Joe. Ashamed, he walked off the set. The credits rolled over the remaining footage and the applause continued unabated, well after they were off the air.

Stay tuned for **The Great Purple Hoo-Ha, Part Two**!

More Laughs!

More Sex!

More Irrelevant Stories!

Aliens! Elvis! Primordial Magick from the Origins of Everything!

Acknowledgements

About twenty years ago, I lived in Poughkeepsie, New York, not far from the locations described in this novel. When I was able to get away from my computer-bound job, I hiked around the waterfront and fantasized about writing a novel set in the old warehouses along the river. That novel was going to be a horror novel – but somehow, with the distance of time, the horror has leached out and been replaced with something much sillier.

So thanks to all the strange, wonderful, creative, creepy and/or mundane people of Dutchess and Ulster Counties in New York's Hudson Valley, and especially to Mark Marinoff, who once told me that he overhead a passenger on the Metro-North train explaining to another that "This is Poughkeepsie. Everyone has a cough or a limp."

The "spinning feelings" technique that Atem uses to sober up Joe in the early part of the novel is based on the Neuro-Hypnotic Repatterning work of Richard Bandler.

Thanks also to the many people, over the years, who have participated in my magick workshops – I've attempted to give some flavor of those experiments among the various tales in this book. Thanks to DJ, who puts up with my literary obsessions. And special thanks to Mogg Morgan at Mandrake of Oxford for buying me lunch and making this happen.

PHF

About the Author

Philip H. Farber is the author of *Meta-Magick: The Book of Atem: Achieving New States of Consciousness Through NLP, Neuroscience and Ritual* (Weiser Books, 2008) and *Futureritual: Magick for the 21st Century* (Eschaton Productions, 1995), a manual of neurological exploration. His articles on magick, consciousness and popular culture have appeared in Green Egg Magazine, The Journal of Hypnotism, Hypnosis Today, Mondo 2000, High Times, Paradigm Shift, Reality Sandwich and other unique publications and web sites. Phil is a Certified Hypnotist and a Licensed Trainer of Neuro-linguistic Programming, with a private practice in New York's Hudson Valley. Visit Phil at www.meta-magick.com.

Learn more about Atem, read:

Meta-Magick: The Book of Atem:
Achieving New States of Consciousness Through NLP, Neuroscience and Ritual
Weiser Books, 2008

"**Meta-Magick** *is a brilliant and patently original book of magical instruction that future generations will revere as an 'ancient classic.'*" - **Lon Milo DuQuette**, author of *My Life with the Spirits* and *Enochian Vision Magick*

Available wherever books are sold.

Ingram Content Group UK Ltd.
Milton Keynes UK
UKHW040605020623
422763UK00001B/41